The Secret of
Saturday Cove

The Secret of Saturday Cove

BARBEE OLIVER CARLETON

ILLUSTRATED BY CHARLES GEER

HOLT, RINEHART AND WINSTON

NEW YORK • CHICAGO • SAN FRANCISCO

*To the boys and girls of Friendship
this book is fondly dedicated
by their friend, the author*

Contents

Chapter

1

JONATHAN'S CHART

Wﾐ ITH an explosion of spray the trap struck the water and settled slowly downward.

The boy in the dory paused, his hand on the throttle. After the noisy throb of the motor the long cove lay as quiet as a dream. The bay was brilliant with summer — blue of the water, green of the island spruces, the bright spark of mica flashing from the rocks. Everywhere the fragrance of rockweed and spruce. Nowhere a sound but the white gulls screaming and the *lap*, *lap*, of water against the dory's hull.

This is lobstering, David thought with warm, new pride. "This is the life!" he said aloud.

Sally sniffed deeply. "It smells kind of nice," she agreed. "But what are we waiting for? I have a feeling we ought to hurry."

David Blake grinned at his young sister seated in the bow. She looked like a figurehead, he decided, chubby though she was in her hated life jacket. Her hair, like his own, was the pale color of beach grass,

1

and like all the Blakes she had eyes as blue as the sea. As usual, she was bouncing with impatience.

"What's your hurry?" he asked. "We're pretty near done."

"You brought me along to help you haul," Sally reminded him. "So let's finish hauling. Then I can tell that stuck-up Poke of yours that I hauled all your traps."

David laughed. "Tell him what?"

"Well, anyway, I helped."

David started up the motor and they moved on down the cove toward the bay. The afternoon was strangely still, and the little motor beat like a slow pulse.

"You're just jealous, Sally," her brother said. "Poke isn't stuck-up, and you know it."

"Well, he's a sissy, then," Sally declared. "If he isn't scared of the water, why doesn't he ever come hauling with you?"

"He just doesn't like it," David said defensively. But he frowned, knowing that she was right. Loving the sea as he did, it was hard to be reminded that his best friend hated it.

Sally pointed suddenly behind him. "Look! Thunderheads!"

David glanced toward the west where the little town of Saturday Cove lay shimmering under the hot July sun. Low over the hills behind the town black clouds boiled up angrily. From the distance came the dull mutter of thunder.

"There are four more traps outside Blake's Island,"

he told her. "We'll have just about time to finish hauling." He speeded up the motor. With a staccato roar the little dory fanned her way through the smooth waters of the cove. Beating sturdily into the tide rip where cross-currents roiled and churned, she entered the broad acres of Penobscot Bay. Here the water was choppy, and David tightened his hold on the stick.

"If the going gets rough," he shouted over the noise of the motor, "we can always go ashore at Blake's and wait out the storm there."

Sally bobbed her tallow braids. "Then I hope it'll be a ripsnorter!" she cried. Perhaps they could even explore the Blake homestead again. Before Poke came to town — that queer and quiet boy that David seemed to like so much — she and her brother had spent wonderful hours together, exploring the islands off Saturday Cove. Secretly, she was glad that Poke had proved to be such a sissy about the water. Now David might see how much fun he could have with her, just the two of them again.

Her brother held the dory steady toward the familiar island that lay off Grindstone Point. As the distance shortened, they caught a glimpse of the house — a proud old pioneer still standing among the wind-twisted spruces on the headland.

David felt a rush of affection for the place. His family still owned Blake's Island, although the house was now used only as a fishermen's refuge. But this whole area — these islands, this cove — was the blood and bone of the Blake family. For it was into this very harbor that John Blake sailed on a Saturday long ago,

3

so naming the inlet and the village that later grew from the wilderness on the mainland. And somewhere in these waters the boy, Jonathan, had rowed secretly, alone and afraid. . . .

"I know what you're thinking," Sally shouted from the bow. "You're thinking about the Blake treasure."

David looked surprised. "Who believes that yarn any more?"

Sally narrowed her eyes thoughtfully. "You do. I heard you pumping Dad about it last night."

David said nothing. He squinted past Sally, on the lookout for the first buoys that lay off the ledges.

"I bet you've stumbled onto something, David Blake!" Suspicion grew fast in Sally's mind, and in no time at all was full-grown.

Silently, David avoided a buoy of Willis Greenlaw's that bobbed in their course.

"And I bet, when I'm not around, you go ashore at Blake's a lot."

David started to whistle to himself.

"And maybe you even *dig*," Sally accused him.

He laughed. "You're wrong there, towhead."

Sally's eyes flared. "You've found out something, I can tell! And I should think you'd let me in on it."

"Girls talk too much."

"Well, when I'm twelve," snapped Sally, "I hope I'll know enough to get help when I need it."

"Why don't you just settle on learning how to swim?" said her brother. "At the rate you're going, you'll be too old to totter down to the beach for your lessons."

Sally bit her lip and looked away, and David felt ashamed. He had struck Sally's weak spot. Each summer she spent hours at the beach taking the lessons offered by the Red Cross or practicing strokes in an old inner tube, but never once daring to put her head underwater. Each summer she had given up in defeat and shame. Now, the subject of swimming was avoided by the Blakes, and Sally, in despair, had begun to hope for a miracle.

"You keep working on your swimming," David added more kindly, "and I'll let you in on something."

"You will?" broke in Sally.

"If and when I need any help," her brother finished firmly.

Disappointed, Sally was about to retort when thunder cracked close by. Southwesterly, beyond Grindstone Point, sea and sky already seemed to meet in a mighty silver rainfall. "It'll be a ripsnorter," Sally told herself, exulting. "I have a feeling. . . ."

David, too, was studying the sky. "Plenty of time," he said. He shut off the motor and drifted close to the red-and-black striped buoy off their starboard side.

Intent, Sally leaned forward. The business of hooking and hauling in the trap never failed to excite her. "Let me try, Dave," she said. She would show him how well a girl could do it.

Seizing the gaff, she made a thrust at the toggle line, and missed. Then, as the dory was about to pass over the line, Sally timed her move deliberately. With one swift stroke of the hook she snared the rope. Triumphant, she dragged the buoy into the dory.

"There!" She looked to her brother for approval.

"Not bad," David said. Then, bracing himself, he hauled in the wet rope, coil over coil, until the trap came over the side, streaming rockweed and water.

"Oh, good." Sally eyed the green-blue catch in the trap. "We've caught three in this one."

But David did not need his iron ruler to note that one was a "short," its main shell under the legal length. Back into the water went the lobster in a dark and shining arc. "Two it is," he corrected. Cautiously, he took one of the creatures between head and flapping tail. Holding first one waving claw, then the other, he pushed a wooden wedge firmly into the joint. This done, he tossed the shellfish into a bushel basket now filled with the day's restless catch.

6

He thrust the other teasingly toward Sally. "How about plugging him for me?"

For a moment Sally hesitated. Then, with a hand not wholly steady, she grasped the second lobster well behind its punishing claws, as David had done. Gingerly, she inserted the plug into one claw, then into the other. When the chore was completed Sally was breathing as hard as if she had been running. Supposing the hideous thing had seized one of her fingers!

As David moved on to the other traps he explained, his voice eager, how a lobster uses his claws as a knife and a fork, one for cutting, one for crushing. Surprised, Sally stared at him. Why, not only did David love lobstering, he even loved these lobsters.

"If they snap off a finger," she told him tartly, "I can't see what difference it makes whether they cut it off or crush it off."

Her brother laughed. "Well, you still have all ten of yours, haven't you? You did fine. If you could stay out of trouble long enough you might even make a good hauling partner someday."

"Thanks," said Sally briefly. But she glowed inside with pride.

Swiftly, David baited the last trap and thrust it into the darkening bay. The motions were growing sure and familiar, but skill had not come overnight. From early boyhood he had gone lobstering out of the cove with his Uncle Charlie.

Then, this summer of his twelfth year, he had done more than that. With a knowledge gained during long hours of helping at Fishermen's Dock, David had caulked and repaired Uncle Charlie's old dory. Almost before the last patch of snow had melted from behind the gear sheds, he and Poke had painted her and stenciled high on her side the name, *Lobster Boy*. Then, his thirty traps and trap heads made ready during the blustering weeks of winter, he was prepared. When the days turned warm and school ended, he, too, ran his own trap line, short though it was, along with Willis Greenlaw and Foggy Dennett and the other lobstermen. With each week that passed David added to his little college fund at the bank. With each day he gained a deeper respect for the sea.

Now, glancing at the sky, he saw that he had delayed too long. In the few brief minutes he had taken to finish running his line the squall had gathered itself

and sprung. Whitecaps fled across the bay like rabbits before the weasel wind. And down in the cove he saw the spray leap high against the channel buoys. There was no longer any choice between the town landing and the nearby island.

"It looks like we make a run for Blake's," he shouted, and he opened the motor wide.

Sally's answer was lost in the quick roar. Dodging the tossing buoys, they made a broad arc around the point. Once beyond the shelter of the ledges, the little dory pitched sharply in the tide rip. Now and again the propeller rose out of water, and the motor coughed and hesitated.

"Don't let her stall," breathed David, and he felt the perspiration gather on his brow. But the motor beat on,

and minutes later they entered the island cove. Throttling back, he ran the dory up onto the shore above the tide line.

Before they had beached and tied her, the rain began. It fell at first in great, cool drops. Then, as they struggled across the slippery ledges, the very heavens seemed to open.

"Hurry up," gasped David. He caught his sister's wet hand and half dragged her through the spruces. Past the dim shape of the barn they raced, and down the path where grass slapped wet against their legs. Before them stood the house — foursquare and silver-gray in the rain. With a thrust of his shoulder, David forced open the creaking door. Panting, they pushed it shut behind them.

Here was refuge. For, dark and musty though the old kitchen might be, here they were safe from the sea and the wind.

David groped above the wooden sink for the candle and matches he had used before. This time, he thought, he had been lucky. He would not ignore the thunderheads again. He would not trust to luck.

"It's dark in here, isn't it?" Sally whispered. "Spooky, sort of."

"It ought to be, with most of the windows shuttered up. Don't go and get scared now."

"Who's scared?" scoffed Sally. But she remained close beside him as a snarl of thunder echoed through the empty house.

David lighted a candle and thrust it into an old bottle. In the dim light poor Sally's face seemed very pale, her eyes enormous. Maybe he ought to let her in on his discovery, David thought. That would take her mind off the storm, all right. He seized the bottle and held it high. "Come on, Sally. I'm going to show you something."

Instantly, their shadows leaped into giant shapes against the wall. Sally eyed the murky rooms that yawned beyond the kitchen. "N-no, thanks. It's so c-cosy in this nice old kitchen." She settled herself firmly on an overturned nail keg. "Besides, I'm c-cold."

David set the bottle down. "All right. It'll keep." He moved over to the huge fireplace and laid a fire, using the driftwood and paper that he kept ready in the wood box. Often, when it was damp hauling and he was wet and cold, he stopped off at the island and built himself a fire. Occasionally, he knew, the other lobstermen did the same thing. The door was always open.

Sally asked suddenly, "What'll keep? Is it something about the Blake treasure?"

"Could be," said David. Carefully, he poured a little kerosene onto the wood from a can left by one of the men. Let her wonder. It would give her something to think about besides the storm.

Another explosion of thunder. Then the hail began to fall, rattling like birdshot against the shutters.

A cunning gleam came into Sally's eyes. "What makes you think there ever was any treasure in the first place?"

David struck a match and the wood kindled into flame. "Everyone in the family always said there was,

11

for one thing. Dad's father told him about it, and his father told him, and that's the way it went, back two hundred years or more."

"Well, I never did see why they didn't dig it up again."

David shrugged. "Nobody knows. Maybe they couldn't find it."

Sally sniffed. "That's silly. If I buried something, I guess I could find it again. Anyway, why did they want to hide it in the first place?"

"You just want to hear the story again," said David. He pulled a box close to the blaze and Sally moved beside him. Outside, the wind and the hail battered the ancient house. But here in the kitchen the fire crackled and they were warm and content.

"One night," David began, "during the Revolutionary War, John Blake saw a shaving mill come into this cove."

"What's a shaving mill?" asked his sister, not quite remembering.

"Dad says that's what they called the long boats that the British used. Wherever there was a house or a settlement, they would come ashore off their frigates and take whatever they needed."

Sally was indignant. "That was dirty."

"That was war," David said dryly. "Well, one night a band of British came ashore and climbed the path we just came up over. They seized John Blake's musket and they butchered the sheep and cows and made off with what they wanted."

For a moment the two were silent, seeing in the

shadowy kitchen the heavy-booted Redcoats, the children huddled about their mother, the white face of John Blake who, without his firing piece, was helpless to defend his home.

"John's wife, Sally — "

"Sally Blake! Like me," Sally broke in.

David nodded. "Lots of the Blake girls have been named Sally after her. Anyway, the first Sally sent the oldest boy, Jonathan, to hide the valuables — family silver, I think, and pewter, and things like that. And the British never found them."

"Then they might be right here in this house," cried Sally. She seemed not to hear the thunder that crashed and echoed among the islands.

David placed a piece of driftwood on the flames. "But if Jonathan had hidden the things in the house, he could have found them again, couldn't he?"

"I should think so."

"Well, I've been thinking." David faced his sister. "If I had been John and Sally Blake, I'd have stuffed the valuables into something the minute I saw the British drop anchor. Then I'd have sent Jonathan off with them in a boat. Then, when the British came and swarmed all over the house, the valuables would have been safe on some other island. Besides . . ."

"Besides, what?"

David hesitated.

Sally jumped off her keg in a fury. "If you had your precious old Poke here, I bet you'd tell him!"

"Poke doesn't talk."

"Poke does, too, talk." Sally insisted. "Sometimes he

talks exactly like an ency . . . an encyclo . . . a book."

David studied his sister's angry face. Then he laughed. "All right, hothead. Never mind about Poke. Cool off and come on."

David picked up the light and led the way to the buttery, with Sally following closely at his heels. Here it was even darker than the kitchen, and dank with the chill of stone and age. Except for several rusted old lanterns lined up against the wall, the place seemed empty.

David handed Sally the light and stooped to open the door of a low cupboard. "There was a stack of old newspapers in here and I've used them up, building fires. So yesterday I poked around for some more, way in back of this beam."

Sally peered in. "It looks spidery in there."

"And I found this!" David dragged forth a heavy crock. From it he pulled a roll of musty papers.

"Grandfather's charts," he said briefly. "Most of them are like the ones we all use now, except they're too mildewed to be much good."

Sally sniffed with distaste.

"But take a look at this one!" A note of excitement had crept into David's voice.

Her eyes bright, Sally lowered the candle over a stained scrap of canvas that David held flat on the floor. It was a faded and crudely drawn chart. In one corner the name, Jonathan Blake, was written in a childish script.

"It's so old it's all yellow," Sally murmured.

"That's why I studied it. Now look a-here." Tensely,

David's finger traced the rude but certain outlines of Saturday Cove.

Sally crouched, wondering, over the chart.

"Don't go dripping wax all over it," her brother warned. "See. Here's Blake's Island, with a square to mark this house. Then all these little islands with no names on them. But look — " David tapped his forefinger over a small circle. "What do you see?"

"I see a little circle for an island," Sally said unevenly.

"Look in the circle."

Sally looked, and drew in her breath. Very faint, so dim that she could scarcely make it out, she saw the careful cross of a small X.

Chapter

2

AN ENEMY AND AN ISLAND

SALLY looked up, her face aglow. "It's a cross, David! On an island! I'll bet anything it's where Jonathan buried the treasure."

"Could be." Carefully, David rolled up the old chart and tied it with a piece of string from his pocket. "But don't get your hopes up. . . ."

"But why don't we just follow the chart?"

David laughed shortly. "That's easier said than done. It's only a rough sketch drawn by someone who didn't know beans about the cove."

"Jonathan? But Jonathan lived here."

David led the way back to the kitchen. "That's right. But the family had just settled on the island when all this happened, Dad said. They probably hadn't done much scouting around the bay, what with clearing the land and raising the homestead." Thoughtfully, he handed the chart to Sally while he scattered the ashes of the fire. "The cove is drawn too short and the islands are spaced wrong. I recognized Blake's only by the little beach and the square that marks this house.

But anyway it's a good clue. I want Dad and Poke to see it."

"David? Can't I help?" There was no mistaking the longing in Sally's voice.

"Maybe." Her brother snuffed out the candle and flung open the door. "Look, Sally. The storm is over."

They gazed out upon a fresh and shining world. The sun sparkled on the spruces and the spruces breathed in the light wind. For an instant the two stood silent in the doorway. Then David said, "We'd better get going."

Down on the little beach the *Lobster Boy* lay safe but stranded, yards from the ebbing tide. David and Sally removed their shoes and socks and rolled up their jeans. Then they dragged the dory down the flats and into the water.

Soon they were beating their way through the cove toward Fishermen's Dock. Sally, with Jonathan's chart held proudly in her lap, half turned in the bow to watch their progress. As they entered the inner harbor David cut down his speed as usual. They were halfway to the town landing when they noticed the boat — a powerful mahogany inboard, new to the cove. It was roaring away from the yacht club float too fast for courtesy or safety, and it was bearing straight down on them. For a moment David stared, waiting for the other to check his speed, to change his course.

Then he shouted to Sally, "Hold on!" He pushed the stick to starboard as far as he dared, but in a flash the newcomer followed them. For a chilling instant it seemed that the two boats must crash head-on. Then the faster boat shied easily to one side, leaving the little dory pitching crazily in its wake.

David steadied the *Lobster Boy* on her course and said nothing. But his lips pressed angrily together as the tall boy in the other boat shouted, "Quit holding up traffic!" Then, with an insolent burst of power, the cruiser continued out of sight around the point.

Wrathfully, Sally stared after the show-off. "He could have upset us."

David's face was grim. "He practically did." But there was much work to be done and the day was ending. Talk could wait.

With the motor idling, they drew alongside the lobster car, a padlocked floating crate where David kept his catch until he sold it to the hotel. Into this he emptied the day's catch, the mottled shellfish splashing one by one into the dark water.

Sally rinsed out the bait pail, then helped swab the dory, dipping the sponge over the side into the cold water of the harbor. Finally, they had made the *Lobster Boy* fast for the night, and David led the way up the ramp in silence.

A genial, foghorn voice hailed them from the wharf, and they glanced up to see Uncle Charlie. Leaning on a piling and smoking his pipe, he looked as seamed and as comfortable as an old glove.

"How's the haulin'?" he shouted, as if a large expanse of water still separated them.

David grinned and raised his voice. "There's nothing wrong with the hauling, Uncle Charlie. I've averaged one and a half to a trap for 'most a week now."

"No need to yell," bellowed the old lobsterman, and he tinkered cheerfully with his hearing aid. "At thirty-six cents a pound, that ain't hay, is it?"

"I had a good teacher," David told him generously.

"Shucks, son, you're a natural-born salt. Which is a sight more'n I can say for that young trouble-maker that just went out."

Sally was still blazing with indignation. "Did you see what happened?"

Uncle Charlie snorted. "I see the whole thing. That was Roddie McNeill, and somebody ought to paddle him good or else teach him how to act in a boat. Foolin' around like that, and headin' out at this hour."

David frowned. "McNeill? The same Mr. McNeill who bought Grindstone Point from Dad?"

"Ayuh. Same McNeill." Uncle Charlie knocked the ashes out of his pipe. "They're putting up a big house down to the point."

David nodded, bitterly feeling the loss of Blake land. Then Uncle Charlie shouted a fresh bit of news.

"Young Roddie aims to do some haulin', so they say."

Sally broke in, "Hauling! Why, that smarty-cat doesn't know one end of a boat from the other."

"He'll learn," Uncle Charlie said dryly. "Haulin's hard work, and it'll mebbe make a man of him," he added.

David's heart sank at the prospect of Roddie McNeill hanging around the cove. "Where does he keep his boat and his gear?" he asked.

"Likely over to the yacht club." Losing interest, Uncle Charlie put his pipe away. He ignored the town clock that rose above the elms on Main Street and squinted up at the sky. "Close to suppertime. I'll give you young'uns a lift home. But first, step over to the shack a minute. I got something for you." The old lobster-man was pleased with himself. He was about to play Santa Claus. David knew the signs.

Together, the three crossed the wharf and crunched up the clamshell path to the sheds where the lobstermen kept their gear.

The old man had recently given up lobstering in order to tend his antique shop nearby. "Not that I'm gitting too old to haul," he told everyone loudly. "I ain't." And to prove it, he still maintained his gear shed and hauled a few traps whenever he had a hankering for a lobster stew. This gave him excuse enough for spending his spare time around Fishermen's Dock with his pipe and his cronies.

Between the rows of traps piled outside to dry, they approached the old shed, as familiar to the children as home. For they had often gone out with Uncle Charlie when he was lobstering full-time, or passed a foggy morning by his little stove, helping him to mend his gear.

Actually their great-uncle, Charlie Blake had long been their favorite relative. It was from him that David had learned most of what he knew about lobstering. And it was Uncle Charlie who had given David the dory that he had reconditioned into the *Lobster Boy*.

The old man unlocked the door and they entered the sun-pierced gloom of the shed. David sniffed curiously at the smell of fresh paint in the air.

21

"You handling all the gear you can?" yelled Uncle Charlie.

"Not exactly," David admitted. "But I can't line up any more this season."

"Well, son," chuckled Uncle Charlie, "you've got 'em lined up now, fifteen of 'em. Fresh-painted, too." There along the top of Uncle Charlie's bench was a neat row of main buoys — old, but solid and sun-dried. Each had a new coat of red-and-black paint underneath its green tip — David's colors. And each was marked with David's number and his initials.

Speechless, the boy looked at Uncle Charlie whose lean face shone with pleasure.

"Shucks. They's no point in letting this gear just loaf around. You can set these any time you've a mind to. Traps outside to go with 'em."

"Thanks, Uncle Charlie!" David said with all his heart.

"Ayuh," said the old man, embarrassed. "Here's a key. You might's well use the shack, too. They's room enough for the both of us."

Before David could answer, Uncle Charlie changed the subject. "How's the swimming, Sally?"

Sally bit her lip. "I'm — I'm taking lessons at the beach, but . . . ." Her voice trailed away.

Without a word, Uncle Charlie reached up to his top shelf. He handed her a dusty bottle. Inside was a tiny full-rigged ship, complete to the last miniature lifeboat and anchor.

"That's a present ahead of time for learning to swim. You'll learn soon," he promised.

Sally's eyes grew round and slowly filled with happy tears. Unable to speak, she gave the old man a fierce hug.

"Shucks," said Uncle Charlie. "Let's git out of here."

The afternoon air smelled of wild roses growing behind the sheds and of rockweed on the flats.

"Look," Sally cried softly. "The island has David's colors."

Beyond the point lay Blake's Island, richly banded in color. It was green-tipped with spruces above the broad band of red where the dying sun tinted the ledges. And below at the waterline shone the wet black of rockweed. David felt a quick rush of pride. Why, in a way, Blake's Island, owned as it had been by generations of Blakes, was his own.

Uncle Charlie slapped his trousers. "Gitting towards suppertime. Let's git goin'."

The ancient car started up with a hoarse roar, and they jounced away from the docks.

"Speaking of islands," bellowed Uncle Charlie over the racket of the engine, "I hear tell Mr. McNeill wants to buy one off'n the point. I guess all that money of his is burnin' a hole in his pocket."

David felt Sally's elbow dig sharply into his side. Which island contained the old Blake treasure? Suddenly David was impatient to reach home.

They pounded over the bridge at Goose Creek and roared down the narrow road that led north along the shore.

"How many islands your folks own now, David?" bawled Uncle Charlie.

"Just Blake's. And Tub Island, of course, since it's joined to Blake's by a sand bar."

"That's a-plenty," boomed the old man, "taxes bein' what they are."

"You own Blueberry Island and Little Fox, too, don't you?" asked Sally. "I bet you'd never sell them."

"Sell 'em tomorrow for a wooden nickel," chuckled Uncle Charlie. "Sick and tired of payin' the taxes."

But he doesn't mean it, David reassured himself. For, taxes or no taxes, Uncle Charlie was too much of a Yankee trader ever to part with anything without what he called "a good dicker."

They rounded the bend and came to an explosive halt under the elms that sheltered the Blake house.

"Well, it's most suppertime," Uncle Charlie an-

nounced. And with a quick wave, he bounced off in a cloud of dust.

Supper was creamed salt cod and garden peas, and David ate hungrily, listening to Sally's high-flown account of the afternoon's adventures. By the time Mrs. Blake served the rhubarb pie, tart and hot from the oven, Sally had slowed down.

Then David brought up the subject that lay uneasy on his mind. "Dad, have you heard about Mr. McNeill wanting to buy an island?"

Mr. Blake's years of teaching had given him the look of a patient scholar. He looked especially patient, as he sipped his coffee.

"Well, David," he began, "like all the Blakes, you hate to see the land go. But it's bringing a good price now. This is the time to sell. The island costs money each year in taxes, you know."

Shock, like a cold wave, broke over David. He laid down his fork and stared aghast at his father. "But you'd never sell Blake's, Dad. Not Blake's!" Impatiently, he waited for his father's answer.

"Now, David," said his mother gently. "It just isn't sensible to hold onto land that doesn't bring any income. The old house out there is going to ruin. We simply can't afford it. But Mr. McNeill will pay us a fair price. He said that of all the islands in Saturday Cove, his son's first choice is Blake's."

"His son! What does his son want with Blake's?" David broke in. He saw again the contempt on Roddie McNeill's face as he broke the harbor rules for the fun of it.

25

"According to his father, the boy likes to do a little shooting and camping," said Mr. Blake. "And I gather that young McNeill gets pretty much what he wants."

David was silent. He thought of the house and its great fireplace where he could warm himself during cold hauls. This would be Roddie's camp. He thought of the island squirrels that by summer's end would be all but tame — the little shy rabbits that lived in the island woodlot. These would be Roddie's targets.

"And, too, Blake's is the best buy for the McNeills," his father was saying, "since it's the nearest island to their point."

David said bitterly, "*Their* point!"

"The McNeills own it now," his father reminded him. "Times change, David. We can't be sentimental about the land."

Sally had gazed from one of them to the other. Now she burst out, "But what about the Blake treasure? Just when we've found our clue, that man can't go buying up the islands."

"Eat your pie, Sally," said her mother. "That treasure isn't likely to turn up after all this time. And even if it did, it never was money, you know — just household goods that they valued in those days."

Mechanically, David finished supper and gazed through the window at the tulip tree that grew by the gate. In the century since a Blake sea captain had brought it home and planted it there, it had grown strong and beautiful.

The boy took a deep breath. "As far as the treasure goes, I don't think it's on Blake's, anyway. But John

26

Blake's home island ought to be worth more to this family than money."

Mr. Blake raised a quiet brow at his wife, but David missed it. An idea came skyrocketing into his mind, raising with it a high, new hope.

"Dad! Mother!" He faced them earnestly. "It's been good hauling these last few weeks. I'm putting all I planned to into my college fund, and a little more besides. With my new traps I'll have enough extra money by the end of August to pay those taxes myself."

Mrs. Blake rose hastily and murmured something about "seeing to the stove."

Her husband said nothing for a long minute. Then he cleared his throat and looked up. "And what if your good luck doesn't hold, David? What then? Supposing you strike a slack season? Or suppose a storm hits you and you lose your gear?"

David thought this over. Then he said quietly, "I'd like to try it, Dad. I think I can do it."

"You like lobster fishing that well, do you?"

The boy hesitated, then tried to put his thoughts into words. "I love it, Dad. It's the sea, I guess. It's — big. It's never the same for long, but it's always wonderful, and beautiful, and . . . ." David groped for the right word.

"Challenging?"

"That's it!"

Mr. Blake nodded. "You'll find that owning an island will be quite a responsibility. But I don't believe it will prove too big for you." He turned from the gratitude in his son's face and called toward the kitchen.

27

"Ellen! Remind me to see Lawyer Perry tomorrow. We're making over the deed to Blake's Island to one David Blake."

Mrs. Blake returned with hot coffee. She had a tender smile for her husband. "John, what a lovely way to settle things. I didn't want to sell Blake's."

"Neither did I," John Blake declared, and all four laughed with relief.

"If Mr. McNeill wants an island so bad," Sally put in ungrammatically, "Uncle Charlie says he'll sell Little Fox or Blueberry for a wooden nickel."

"What makes you think the treasure isn't on Little Fox or Blueberry?" David asked.

"Perhaps we can tell something from that old chart you found," said Mr. Blake. "Let's have a look at it."

"I held it on my lap all the way in," Sally began. Then she broke off and her eyes went blank.

"Uh-huh," said David, exasperated. "You left it in Uncle Charlie's gear shed."

But Sally's hand had gone to her mouth in horror. "I had it on my lap. I kept it safe on my lap all the way in to the cove." Stricken, she turned to her brother. "Oh, David," she wailed. "I never once had it in the shed. When you yelled, 'Hold on' when that Roddie McNeill headed into us, it must have been then . . . ."

David stared at her in disbelief. "Do you mean to say you lost that chart overboard?"

Sally, unable to answer, bit her lip and nodded.

David rose to his feet and pushed back his chair roughly. Anger darkened his face, and scorn for Sally tightened his voice. "I turn up the first clue to the treasure that this family's ever had, and you go lose it overboard like a ninny. It serves me right. That's what I get for trusting a girl. If it had been Poke, this wouldn't have happened."

A painful lump filled Sally's throat and the world swam in a sea of shame.

"I'm off to see Poke," David told his parents shortly.

Without looking again at Sally, or seeing the misery in her face, he slammed the door behind him.

Chapter

3

PROWLER ON THE DOCK

THE road south to Saturday Cove winds and wheels and tacks with the shoreline as if it had all the time in the world. But as everyone in town knew, there was a short cut. The old wood road turned off at Goose Creek and struck through the woods to Harbor Road, and thence to town.

Hot with anger, David took the short cut. Give a girl something special to take care of, he told himself, and what's the first thing she does? Loses it. But Poke would know what to do, he thought, and he quickened his stride.

His steps echoed loudly over the planks that bridged the creek. Here in the woods it was very dark. Little of the starlight entered this deep and silent growth. With difficulty, David made his way along the uneven ruts. Low branches slapped against his face and his feet slipped on the mossy stones. I should have brought a flashlight, he thought.

Suddenly, he stopped to listen. Was someone else walking this way? He paused, hoping for company.

But he heard nothing. Only the fifes of the peepers in the bog and the low, slow, steady drumming of bull-frogs.

From nearby rose the shrill squeal of some small creature, mouse or mole, and after a silence the low, triumphant hooting of the hunter owl. A swift chill raised the hair on the back of David's neck, and he hurried on.

When the first of the street lights winked welcome at him from Harbor Road, David glanced back into the darkness. There was, after all, no whisper of foot-steps, nobody at all behind him. The woods were silent. With relief David left them behind.

On Main Street he passed several of the lobstermen whom he saw daily around the docks. They looked unfamiliar dressed in suits instead of the woolen gar-ments and rolled boots of their trade. But their friendly, man-to-man greetings filled David with pleasure. "See you 'round," they called to him.

I'm one of them, he thought, with a quick surge of pride.

He turned in at the Harbor Supply where Poke often kept store for his uncle, Fred Kibbe, who owned it. Vigorously he flung open the screen door.

"Quiet, please." Poke's uncombed head was bent low over a large volume open on the counter. His voice sounded faraway in whatever land his mind was roving.

David smiled. Poke Stokes' voice did not match Poke at all. It was round and powerful, while Poke himself resembled a spindle buoy, spare of frame and taller than

31

other boys his age. His thin face was a study of serious-
ness, and his dark eyes were grave. "Poker Face,"
someone in school had dubbed him when he first came
to town two years before. And Poke, David was sure,
had encouraged the nickname, for he had been chris-
tened Elijah and he hated it.

"Listen to this," Poke began in what Sally called his
"lecture voice." "It says here that the horseshoe crab
is not a crab at all."

David grinned, feeling better already. "I've stayed awake nights, wondering."

"It is first cousin to the scorpion," Poke informed him soberly. "In the South Sea Islands the natives use its shell as a soup ladle."

"What's the tail used for?"

Poke's dark eyes widened. "A spearhead, naturally. In order to fill the soup kettle, you see."

David wagged his head. "With you around, I don't

know why I bother to save money for college. Sally says you talk just like a book."

Poke's hungry face lighted into a rare smile. "She does? Sally says that?"

David nodded, relieved that a group of tourists entered at that moment to buy soft drinks. Sally had said other things, too, about Poke. Jealous things. It was unpleasant, having to hide Sally's growing jealousy from his best friend. David studied the latest assortment of postcards, wondering why he bothered to hide it at all.

Then, suddenly, he knew why. Poke lived alone with his uncle, and seldom mentioned his parents who were not living. But whenever he did speak of them his face held the same wistful pleasure as when he was at David's house talking with Mr. and Mrs. Blake, or teasing Sally in his sober fashion. In a way, Poke had made David's family his own.

The screen door shut behind the tourists. David looked up to find Poke's brown eyes regarding him intently.

"What's the trouble, Dave?"

"It's troubles, plural," David shrugged. "Sally. And a lost chart. And an island with a family treasure hidden on it — somewhere in the cove. And a man who wants to buy an island — somewhere in the cove."

Poke's eyes began to gleam with interest. There was nothing he enjoyed so much as working out the answer to a difficult problem. "Let's go sit down and hear the facts. It's stuffy in here."

On the wharf outside was a line of battered old

wicker chairs. Here, during the day, Poke's Uncle Fred could often be found in company with one or several of his customers. In the afternoon sun these chairs were a favorite gathering place for the men when they came in from hauling.

The two boys made themselves comfortable outside the Supply windows, where they could keep an eye on the store.

"Where's your Uncle Fred?" asked David, propping his feet on a weather-worn pile.

Poke nodded toward Dennett's Boat Shed, a neighboring structure which seemed to have grown out of the odds and ends of boats built there in the past. "He's helping Perce Dennett on the new seiner. I'm supposed to call him if I get stuck. But I never get stuck," added Poke simply. "Now, tell me all."

So David shared with Poke the events of the past two days — his discovery of Jonathan's treasure chart and Sally's loss of it, the near accident in the cove because of Roddie McNeill, Roddie's plans to go lobstering and Mr. McNeill's intention of buying an island off Saturday Cove, Uncle Charlie's gift of the gear, and, finally, David's new ownership of Blake's Island.

Poke held up a hand and shook his head happily. "As I see it, you have just four little problems: Blake's Island, the treasure chart, Sally, and the McNeills."

"*Little* problems!" David scoffed.

Poke ignored him. "First, that's great news about Blake's Island. Earning the tax money should be easy with Uncle Charlie's extra traps. There's no problem there. As long as you keep on hauling, that is."

"I'll keep hauling, all right," David assured him. He hesitated, then he said, "If you'd go partners with me, Poke, it would be a cinch. We could set out a lot more traps. . . ."

Poke turned his face away from David and gazed across the cove where the tall riding lights of the sailboats were dancing on the tide. "You're doing all right, Dave. You don't need a partner." Then he turned back, changing the subject, "I'd like to have seen that chart. But why worry about losing it since it was inaccurate? Seeing the X is enough. That proves that *something* was buried *somewhere*."

"But where?" said David hopelessly.

"Easy. Find out how long Jonathan was gone that night."

"How long Jonathan was gone?" Hope and bewilderment mingled in David's face. But before Poke could explain, the screen door slammed.

"Customer," Poke said briefly. He unfolded his long legs and went inside. David followed.

It was Foggy Dennett, and he grinned when he saw the boys blinking in the bright lights of the store. "You boys workin' hard out in them rockin' chairs?" he teased. "Give us a dozen root beers, Poke. It's hotter than fury in that boat shed."

David helped Poke put the cold bottles into a bag for the lobsterman. Much as he liked Foggy, he hoped his visit would be brief. He was impatient to learn what Poke had meant.

"How is your brother's seiner coming along?" Poke was asking.

"Comin' good. We haul most the day and go to boat-building the rest the time." Foggy laughed good-humoredly. "Come over and give us a hand next week, Dave. We'll be doin' some painting."

"Thanks, I'd like to," David said. He had watched the men the day they laid the keelson, a day when it had been too windy to haul. It was an honor, he felt, to be asked to join them. "I'll have to come some evening, though," he added, "since I haul afternoons."

"Come when you can. Only, why don't you haul mornings like the rest of us, Dave?" Foggy asked curiously. "It's calmer."

"I help with the work around home mornings," David explained. "We have chickens and a garden, and Dad tutors mornings all summer."

"That so?"

"It's easier all around if I haul afternoons."

"You can't kid me," said Foggy with a genial wink at Poke. "Four o'clock's too early for you." He slapped extra coins down on the counter. "You boys have a couple drinks on me."

Back on the wharf the boys gratefully drank their root beers.

"What's all this about how long Jonathan was gone?" David demanded.

"Once you know how long he was away from Blake's," said Poke simply, "you can figure out which island he went to. Starting from Blake's, you can row out to the other islands. Time yourself."

David yelped with joy. "Poke, that's it! You've got

37

it!" Then he grew sober. "Only how can we ever find out a thing like that? It all happened way back during the Revolution."

"Mira Piper," said Poke calmly. "Over at the Historical Society, Mira Piper has all sorts of old books and records. I've read some of them. She knows everything there is to know about this town's past — and present," he added. "She'll be glad to help us."

"All right. Then say we do find out how long he was gone," said David, his mind racing ahead to possibilities. "Next, you and I will row off the distances from Blake's, and somewhere, Poke, we'll find ourselves a treasure." David pursed his lips into a lighthearted whistle.

Poke shook his head. "I shall be honored to dig through the records with you. But count me out of those rosy plans in the dory."

"Why not come along?" David asked lightly.

Poke matched his tone to David's. "No, thanks," he said, as lightly. "Now for Problem Number Three. Sally. But Sally is really no problem."

"Sally's trouble," said David, tolerantly enough.

"Suppose she does rush into things and make mistakes," Poke conceded. "She means well, and she's not afraid like most girls."

"I suppose," said David.

"According to the law of averages, she can't help doing some things right. I'd let her in on the treasure hunt. Besides," Poke glanced at David, "she thinks you're pretty special, you know."

Poke had a wishful look about him as if he were

waiting to hear that Sally thought Poke pretty special, too.

But David said hastily, "Okay. We'll let Sally tag along." Then he changed the subject. "What about the McNeills?"

"If Roddie McNeill makes a good lobsterman, you'll like him well enough. If not, you won't have to worry about him. He'll quit."

"Oh, he'll quit soon enough. But until he does, just let him keep out of my hair."

"Maybe you should tell him politely how to behave in a boat," grinned Poke.

"I'd be the last one he'd listen to. Dad told me Blake's was the island Roddie especially wanted his father to buy. Wait till he finds out I'm the one who kept him from getting it. Next time he may not stop at just showing off."

Poke whistled. "Worse still, wait till he finds out you're the new owner. He'll be so furious he'll probably make off with your bait barrel."

Both boys laughed at the thought of Roddie stealing away with David's enormous barrel of redfish.

"Now for the last problem," said Poke, leaning back in his chair. "So Mr. McNeill wants an island, does he? That's more difficult. Because, of course, now that he can't buy Blake's, he might buy the very island where the treasure is hidden. Tell me, Dave, which islands are for sale?"

"Well, Blake's is mine now, and Tub is connected with Blake's. Big Fox is owned by the government. That leaves Little Fox and Blueberry. Mr. McNeill will probably try to buy one of those when he finds out Blake's isn't for sale."

"Who owns Little Fox and Blueberry?"

"Uncle Charlie. And he'd be happy to sell them both — for a good price."

"Then the answer is simple," Poke declared. "Talk Uncle Charlie into holding onto those islands, at least until you learn where Jonathan went that night."

"Sounds easy," David smiled. "Anyway, thanks, Poke. No more problems."

"Time will tell," said Poke in his deep voice.

The boys fell into a comfortable silence. The rising tide lapped softly against the piles. Now and then faint voices came from Main Street, and across the water from a lighted cabin cruiser drifted the sound of laughter. Under the starry sky the long cove widened into the bay and the bay reached out to the end of the world. It seemed to David that he and his friend were alone on the earth with the summer night and the sea.

"Poke, tell me something." In the light from the window David's blue eyes challenged Poke's brown ones. "How come you never go out hauling with me? How come no one's able to get you into a boat?"

The familiar shadow darkened Poke's eyes and sharpened his face. For a moment he seemed almost a man, already grown up, with a grim knowledge unknown to his friend. David felt uneasy.

"Skip it, Dave," he said quietly.

"Okay, Poke." David found his heart pounding with relief. He could ask Fred Kibbe. He could find out easily enough what Poke's trouble was, if he wanted to. But he knew now that he never would. It was Poke's affair, and someday Poke would tell him.

A stealthy movement nearby interrupted David's thought. While he was wondering what it had been, it was followed by the thud of falling cartons in the shadows beyond the Supply.

"Over by the gas pumps," Poke murmured.

Then they heard the sudden swift pounding of running feet in the solid darkness beyond them. Poke, with David close behind, leaped away from the light of the windows and clattered across the wharf in blind pursuit. David stumbled and Poke paused to help him to his feet.

"Go on!" cried David.

"It's no use," Poke panted. "He's in there by the warehouses. We'd never find him now."

The lane between the docks stretched emptily toward the water on one side, and on the other entered Main Street in a dark jumble of warehouses and boat sheds.

Disappointed, they turned back toward the Supply.

"Now why would anyone want to listen to our corny conversation?" David's voice was puzzled. "Do you suppose he was waiting to sneak into the Supply?"

"Or away from it." Hastily, Poke brushed past him into the store and went at once to the cash register. "Nothing has been touched here," he reported with relief. Then he glanced toward the front door that opened toward Main Street. When Foggy Dennett had left, he had slammed it shut behind him. Now, it was swinging noiselessly back and forth in the light breeze.

David followed his gaze. "Somebody's been in here."

"The plot thickens," said Poke happily. "Anyway, as far as I can see, nothing has been touched."

At this point Mr. Kibbe came in, his cheerful face streaked with sawdust. "How did things go, Poke?"

Briefly, Poke told his uncle of the incident.

"Well, I didn't see anyone coming out." Mr. Kibbe, too, examined the cash drawer. "Nothing's missing. It must have been some kids running around. You can go home now, Poke. I'll be along later."

The boys left the Supply and turned onto Main Street.

"Come on home with me and spend the night," David urged as they approached Poke's street. "You can call your uncle from the house. Besides, I think maybe you need a bodyguard. You have any enemies?"

"Not a one. How about you?"

"Just Sally, and she'll get over it. Come on, Poke, how about it? It's pitch dark and I'd worry all the way home."

"About me?" Poke asked dryly.

"Nope," David admitted. "About me."

"Right. I'll come."

As they turned up Harbor Road David wondered how it would be to live with an uncle who didn't very much care what you did or where you went. He decided that it wouldn't be especially good.

"Tomorrow," Poke announced, "I'll sleep and I'll sleep and I'll sleep."

"You'll sleep nothing," laughed David. "You'll help me feed the chickens. And then, off to the Historical Society."

"Mira Piper," said Poke, "get out your records."

"What do you think our chances are?" David asked suddenly. "I mean of finding out how long Jonathan was gone that night."

"We'll soon know," Poke told him. They passed under the last of the street lights and David smiled. For Poke's face was flushed with excitement.

Avoiding the short cut, they walked home along the shore road. The houses gave way to lonely fields, and the fields to misty marshland. Somewhere, deep in the woods, the owl screeched again.

They walked quite fast and they did not look behind them once.

Chapter

4

SALLY AND POKE

IN spite of his threat to sleep all day Poke was out
of bed with the first savory updraft of bacon and
flapjacks.

"A-hunting we will go," he rumbled, pulling his
clothes over his thin body. "We'll catch a fox and put
him in a box, and then we'll let him go-ho-ho . . . ."
He ran a comb through his dark hair with a fine dis-
regard for direction.

Sodden with sleep, David watched from the opposite
bunk.

"Awake, Blake," Poke said dramatically. "The hunt
is on!"

"Wha' for?" muttered David.

"Facts," declared Poke. "Facts, and maybe a fox.
We'll hunt through the records for facts about the
British raid on Blake's. But we'll also keep an eye out
for that fox that spied on us last night."

David swung his feet out of bed. By the time he
was fully awake and dressed, he had caught Poke's
enthusiasm. This very day they might solve the ancient

mystery of the Blake treasure, as well as the new puzzle of who, last night, was spying on them, and why.

But Mrs. Blake had other plans for them.

She placed before the boys a platter of hot flapjacks, puddled and streaming with honey-butter. Then she reminded David that the lawn could not wait another day and that the garden must be attended to. "Maybe Poke will help," she suggested, as she brought them crisp bacon from the stove.

Gratefully, Poke started heaping his plate. "Mrs. Blake, I am at your service," he assured her. "Anything you want done today I'll do." Then, sighing with pleasure, he attacked his breakfast.

But David protested. "Poke and I had business downtown this morning, Mom. Can't the lawn wait?"

"Dad is tutoring," his mother reminded him, "so it's up to us to keep ahead of things here at home. I've already seen to the chickens," she added, "so you will be free to go hauling after lunch." Her voice was pleasant but firm, and David knew better than to argue.

That does it, thought David. The Historical Society would have to wait. He shrugged and fell to eating.

"Where are Dad and Sally?" he asked after a moment. He was eager to show Sally that he had forgiven her.

"Dad is already at school, and Sally is sleeping off her late hours," smiled his mother. "I'm glad she decided to follow you last night, David. She was so upset about losing the old chart."

David and Poke exchanged a swift glance. David's, puzzled, said, But she wasn't with me. So where did

45

she go? And Poke's warned, Careful. Don't worry your mother until we find out.

A merry staccato sounded on the stairs as Sally came clattering down to breakfast. "Good morning, everybody," she sang. Ignoring the empty chair beside Poke, she took her father's place.

"Did you sleep well, Poke?" she asked, in a voice as sweet as the honey-butter.

Poke choked a little on a piece of bacon. "Fine, thanks," he answered hoarsely. Sally was not in the least surprised to see him. But how did she know he had spent the night here, unless . . . .

David's expression finished the thought. Unless she had seen them coming in together. Unless it was Sally who had spied on them at the wharf.

"We had a telephone call last night," Mrs. Blake was saying, "from Mr. McNeill."

David stopped eating. "About Blake's Island?" he asked.

David's mother smiled at his anxiety. "Your father said that it's no longer for sale. But he told Mr. McNeill that one of the other islands might be bought from Uncle Charlie. Dad plans to have the deed to Blake's made over to you today, David," she added.

"Thanks, Mom," he said simply, and a world of gratitude lay behind the words.

Sally's face was remote and closed. She's all riled up, thought David. Yet, as the boys went outside to work, Sally was humming over the dishes.

"Nobody could look that mysterious without knowing *something*," David grumbled. Frowning, he pushed the lawn mower into position on the sun-dappled lawn. "She skipped out last night, Poke. She's never done that before."

"I shouldn't worry about it." Poke clipped around the tulip tree. "Sally's just jealous. First, you told her that she could help you with the treasure hunt. Then she lost the chart and you probably gave her what-for."

"I did," David admitted.

"Then you let me in on the hunt, not Sally, and it's easy to see what happened next. She felt left out so she followed you to the wharf, she listened to us, she ran. Therefore, Sally is the fox. How's that for reasoning?"

David leaned against the handle of the lawn mower. "Pretty good." Then he remembered something. "Wait a minute, Poke. She got her sneakers soaked, out hauling with me yesterday, so she wore her sandals last night. I remember seeing them at supper."

"So?" Then Poke whistled. "Aha! I see what you mean. Whoever went pounding across the wharf last night was wearing sneakers. You could tell by the sound. So, question one, If it wasn't Sally, who was our fox? And question two, Where was Sally last night?"

"Well, she knows one of those answers, anyway."

"Probably both," said Poke. "She looks as pleased with herself as a cat."

"We could ask her," David said moodily. "But that wouldn't do any good."

"Leave her to me," said the older boy suddenly. "I'll find out."

David looked doubtful. He would hate to see Poke's

47

feelings hurt, and Sally had a tongue like a gaff when she chose to use it.

"I have a way with kid sisters," Poke added, "even the jealous ones."

"Okay, go ahead," said David. "Only how will you get her alone?"

"I'll think of something." Poke returned to his clipping and David, with an eye on the door, tackled the lawn.

But Sally stayed inside all morning to help her mother make preserves. Then, at noon, Mrs. Blake brought the boys a basket of lobster sandwiches and bottles of cold, homemade root beer.

"It's hot in the house," she told them. "How about taking this up to Lookout Rock?"

It was a splendid idea. But there was no sign of Sally.

"You'll be leaving to haul before long, so you had better not wait for Sally." Then his mother said wryly, "She may catch up with you. You never can tell about her."

Lookout Rock was the ledge that crowned the steep rise at Goose Creek. Here David could see across the broad, bright bay to where Dark Harbor lay low on the sea line. On one side he could look down upon his own house and barn and garden, and on the other, the town, with its long inlet white-dotted with lobster boats. It was the top of the little world of Saturday Cove.

Today, Lookout Rock lay drenched in sunlight. High overhead a few sea gulls drifted on an offshore

breeze. Tied up at the yacht club float lay a sleek mahogany inboard.

"Look, Poke." David pointed to a lobster boat that had come alongside one of the many little ledges outside the cove. Its motor could be heard quite clearly from where they sat. "That's Foggy Dennett, hauling outside The Graves."

Poke's interest sharpened. "Funny. He seems to be spending a long time on just one trap."

"He probably has a good catch. The lobsters are really starting to crawl these days," said David with satisfaction. "And out there, just coming in by the point, that's Willis Greenlaw."

"You like the men, don't you, Dave?" Poke asked him.

"Sure. They're mighty nice to me. Foggy's brother didn't even want to charge me full price for my bait. But I'm hauling and making a profit, too. I'm one of them."

Poke nodded. "When are you going to set your new traps?"

"I'll get most of them set today if I start early enough." David turned briskly to the lunch basket. "Let's eat."

Up here there were no problems. They finished their meal in contented silence. Sally still had not come. Finally, they started down.

"You coming back to town with me?" David asked.

Poke shook his head. "I'll stay here for a while in case your mother wants anything done. I may have a word with Sally yet," he said artfully.

"I wish you luck," David grinned. "See you at the Supply." With a quick wave he was off on his bicycle for Saturday Cove.

And luck was with Poke. For not long after he had returned to his clipping on the lawn, Sally joined him.

"I have to run an old errand for Mother," she stated stiffly, "and I'm supposed to go along with you, Elijah."

"Charmed," said Poke, wincing. "I was hanging around, hoping you'd come out."

"Really?" said Sally doubtfully.

"Really. Wait till I put the clippers away and thank your mother."

Sally waited for him, swinging back and forth on the gate. For a time the two walked in silence along the sunny road. Then Poke glanced at Sally. "I certainly admire a girl with spunk enough to do what you did last night."

Sally stared. "How did you know?"

Poke winked at her in answer. He tried to look as if he knew exactly what Sally had done.

"I just wanted to hear what David would tell you about the chart," she said defensively. "And what you'd say about it."

So it was Sally who had spied on them after all. "I don't blame you a bit," Poke assured her. "You were in on the hunt at the beginning. When you lost the chart, you wanted to make up for it, possibly by finding the treasure all by yourself." A glance at her face showed him that he had guessed right. "You needed more facts, so you went after them. Exactly the way a good detective would have done it."

51

Sally was relieved. "Honest?"

"Honest," said Poke stoutly. "That took nerve."

"I like doing things that take nerve," Sally confided. "Especially when they're all over."

They were deep along the old wood road where it was cool and quiet. Sally shuddered, remembering. It was about here that she had heard the owl hoot. But now, with Poke, she felt safe.

"Poke," she said after a moment. "You know what?"

"Nothing would surprise me," Poke said solemnly.

"When you thought you were chasing me last night, you weren't. Because I scooted through the Supply and went home."

Poke stared at her.

"Roddie McNeill was there, too, hiding behind the gas pumps. He heard every word you said — all about the treasure and the islands, and trying to find out how long Jonathan was gone that night, and everything."

Poke's long face darkened. And everything! As if it were not bad enough that Roddie now knew as much about the treasure as they did, he had also overheard their low opinion of him. And he knew of David's pleasure at keeping Blake's Island out of McNeill hands. Perhaps David was right. Perhaps Roddie was the kind to cause trouble.

Sally looked miserable. "I wasn't even going to tell," she said in a low voice. "I thought if Roddie found the treasure first, it would serve David right for the things he said at the table last night."

The silence lengthened until they reached town. Then she touched Poke's arm a little timidly. "You know what I think?"

"I can't imagine," he said dryly.

"I think Roddie found our chart. And I think he hung around last night to see what it was all about. And I think we ought to see Uncle Charlie about not selling Mr. McNeill one of his islands. Because if the treasure isn't on Blake's, it might be on Little Fox or Blueberry."

"Sally," said Poke, who had already come to the same conclusion, "what would we do without you?"

Sally's world was right side up again. Peacefully, she trotted along Main Street at Poke's side.

"How about David?" asked Poke. "We don't want to pay a visit to Uncle Charlie without him."

"David'll never forgive us if we let Uncle Charlie sell his islands," Sally told him earnestly.

"Maybe Uncle Charlie will have something to say about that," Poke said.

The antique shop was a converted boat house, built on the piling above the tide near Fishermen's Dock. A large sign swung lightly overhead, The Lobster Pot — Antiques.

Uncle Charlie sat by the open window overlooking the cove, threading old buttons onto squares of cardboard by means of pipe cleaners.

"Come on in out of the sun," he roared cheerfully. "What you young'uns got on your mind?"

Sally edged carefully around a table laden with old glass. "We came to ask what you're going to do about your islands."

"Islands?" Uncle Charlie boomed. "Going to sell 'em, I hope. T. J. McNeill called me up last night. He's coming in to talk business 'most any minute now." Then he added, "Why?"

Sally glanced unhappily at Poke and took a deep breath. "Uncle Charlie, we found an old chart of Saturday Cove, and one of the islands had a cross marked on it."

"That so? Well, what do you know? Which one?"

"We don't know, sir," put in Poke. "The chart was not accurate. But we think it could have been either Little Fox or Blueberry. If so, that's where the Blake treasure may be hidden."

Uncle Charlie was disappointed and returned to his buttons. "Oh, shooty, that confounded treasure again!

Never did put any stock in all that foolishness. Anyway, I'd git a sight more for an island than I'd git for them pewter spoons. If they ever was any in the first place, which I doubt."

"But Uncle Charlie," Sally wailed just as the shop door opened and a man and woman entered. The woman seemed to fade colorlessly away into the background.

It was the man, also a stranger, who claimed their attention. Very large, very well-dressed, he appeared to fill the shop. He ignored Sally and Poke and addressed himself directly to Uncle Charlie.

"T. J. McNeill," he stated, introducing himself. "You Charles Blake?"

Uncle Charlie could not rise, his lap being filled with buttons and pipe cleaners. But he pushed the ancient lobsterman's cap well back on his shaggy old head and considered the question. Finally he nodded, "Ayuh."

Sally nudged Poke. T. J. McNeill was about to get the "old salt" treatment that worked so well in the antique business.

Seeing only a rather small old man with a mild voice and a lap full of buttons, Mr. McNeill promptly dropped the "Mr." "Well, Blake," said he in a no-nonsense manner, "as I told you last evening on the phone, I am interested in buying your islands, both of them. I am prepared to offer you a fair price — three thousand dollars apiece. And I might add that I am not interested in dickering. I have no time for that sort of thing." He waited, tapping his fingers on the table.

"Come again?" piped Uncle Charlie. "I'm deafer'n a haddock."

Sally gasped. In the shop Uncle Charlie always kept his hearing aid tuned up so that he could hear a foghorn ten miles away.

In a huge bellow, Mr. McNeill repeated the entire speech. When he had finished he was panting. He looked a little less important now than when he had come in.

Uncle Charlie hissed thoughtfully through his teeth and Sally's shoulders began to shake with merriment. Why, Uncle Charlie isn't going to sell the islands at all, she thought. He is just having a little fun with Mr. McNeill.

"Well, now," Uncle Charlie said peevishly. "I don't know as I want to sell them islands, come right down to it. They been in the family since Jonah was a boy."

Mr. McNeill drew breath for another attack. "Come, Blake," he argued, tapping the table until the Sandwich glass jingled. "Land is bringing a good price now. This is the time to unload it, you know."

"I heard ye, McNeill," complained Uncle Charlie, rubbing his ear. "Forty-five hundred dollars each, take it or leave it. Never dicker, myself."

Mr. McNeill's face turned a dark red. "Four thousand each, and not a penny more," he roared.

"Sold, by gosh!" bawled Uncle Charlie happily.

Stunned, Sally stared at Uncle Charlie. He had sold the islands to Mr. McNeill. Both of them. Both Little Fox and Blueberry.

Then her low spirits lifted a little as the old man

added, "I'll have them deeds drawn up in a week or two, soon's I git to it."

"A week or two? Have them deeds, I mean, have those deeds drawn up immediately," ordered Mr. Mc-Neill. "I'm a very busy man." He glanced irritably toward the woman who was standing in front of the case of antique buttons. "Come on, Evelyn," he snapped.

"Thomas," the woman began timidly, "couldn't we buy one of these pewter buttons? I've wanted one for my collection for a long time."

But her husband did not appear to hear her, and Mrs. McNeill turned wistfully away from the antique buttons and followed him through the shop. Poor woman, thought Sally with pity.

Roddie McNeill was leaning against the door.

"I thought I told you to wait in the car, Rod," said Mr. McNeill, but there was only affection in his voice.

Roddie shrugged. "I got bored."

"I hear you're trying your hand at lobstering, son," called Uncle Charlie, kindly enough. "How they crawling?"

Roddie glanced at Uncle Charlie. "They weren't," he said shortly. "But they are now."

Mr. McNeill said smoothly, "Roddie's new at this business and he had poor results at first, of course. But with that boat I bought him and all that fancy equipment, he's beginning to haul them up. He'll be top man in no time, no question about it."

"Ayuh," said Uncle Charlie. "Only they's a sight more to haulin' besides buyin' boats and gear. You git

58

Dave Blake to show you the ropes, son. He's a young-'un, too, but he's haulin' right along with the best of 'em. You'll do good, with Dave around."

Roddie's glance shot toward Poke. Dislike, and something else, glittered in the look. "I'll do better *without* David Blake, thanks."

"Makes no never-mind to me," declared Uncle Charlie loudly. "Only, takes a while to catch on, alone."

"For some, I expect, but not for this one." His good humor restored, Mr. McNeill clapped his son confidently on the shoulder and opened the door. "I tell Rod it's every man for himself in this world. It's a race to the finish, and the smart operator makes his own short cuts or he gets left."

Roddie shrugged his father's heavy hand away. "Don't worry. I'm on to a trick or two." Then, defiantly, he asked, "Aren't you going to get Mother that button she wants?"

"Button?" His father's voice was short. "She's too busy to fool around with buttons."

The door closed sharply behind the McNeills.

Uncle Charlie shook his head. "That young'un's having hard haulin', pleasin' that father of his. And it looks to me like the wife give up trying."

But Sally was no longer interested in Roddie's parents. "I'm glad you got a nice price for your islands, Uncle Charlie," she told him politely. "But if the treasure is on Little Fox or Blueberry, we'll never be able to get it now." Her voice wavered alarmingly.

Uncle Charlie snorted. "Fiddlesticks! You kids go right ahead an do your diggin'. It'll be three, four days before the McNeills own them islands because I'll clean put off seeing the lawyer." He grinned and waved off their thanks.

Relieved and grateful, Sally and Poke hurried outside into the sun.

"Let's do your errand," Poke suggested, heading back toward Main Street. "Then you can wait with me at the Supply until Dave gets back in."

Sally nodded. "Wait till he hears that the McNeills are buying Little Fox and Blueberry."

"Wait until he hears that it was Roddie who spied on us last night," said Poke, and he lengthened his stride. "Too bad it's too late to go to the Historical Society now. We three will need to move fast."

Sally's eyes fairly shone with pleasure. Poke had said, We three. "But we have four whole days," she reminded him. "Uncle Charlie said so. Four days is a long time."

Poke shook his head. "A day to learn how long Jonathan was gone, a day or two to row and measure distances, a day or two to dig. That's cutting it close." He was like a hound following a difficult trail.

Sally trotted faster, and faster still, to keep up with him. "I have the funniest feeling," she confided.

"Possibly an ant down your neck," Poke teased her.

Sally tossed her golden braids. "I have a feeling," she panted, "that tomorrow we'll discover something. You wait and see!"

Chapter

5

"A-HUNTING WE WILL GO!"

MORNING came to Saturday Cove, and with it the heaviest fog of the summer. Sally, peering through the side lights of the front door, could scarcely make out the tulip tree by the gate.

David handed her a set of oilskins. "We're meeting Poke at the Historical Society at nine-thirty. Let's go."

Through a silent world of white they walked in to town. The fragrance of bayberry and spruce was everywhere heavy about them. Now and then a crystal drop gathered and splashed downward through the branches. Sometime in the night the bay and its familiar islands had vanished. From Harbor Road at the head of the town they could see only the ghostly oneness of sea and sky and land. Over it all moaned the dismal voice of the foghorn on Big Fox Island.

Sally mimicked it. "*OOOOOOO-ooo, OOOOOOO-ooo.* Spooky old thing."

"It's a thick fog, all right," said David. "You could slice it with a bread knife."

"But it's a perfect day to read through the old records. I just know we're going to find out how long Jonathan was gone that night the British came. I feel it in my bones." Sally ducked, laughing, as a bluejay took flight from a pine tree and showered them with a cascade of silver drops.

"Let's hope so," said David. "But even if we do find out, we won't be doing any rowing today."

Sally stared at her brother. "But we have to. We haven't much time. Poke said so," she declared as if that settled it.

David shook his head. "We'll have to wait till the fog lifts."

"But you've gone out in a fog before."

"Maybe in a light fog," he agreed. "But not in a pea-soup fog like this. The only times most of us don't haul are in a real good wind, or in a pea-souper."

Sally squinted up at the white sky. There was not a glimmer of sun. "Then it's got to burn off," she said fiercely. "Because in a few days that Roddie McNeill will own Little Fox and Blueberry, both of them, and then where'll we be?"

"No worse off than we were before, probably. There's Poke, coming out of the drugstore."

Poke greeted them, his dark brows drawn together into a puzzled frown. "I was drinking a milk shake while waiting for you two," he told them, "when who should come in but Foggy Dennett and Willis Greenlaw."

"What's wrong with that?" asked David.

"There's nothing wrong, really, except what Willis said, or possibly the way he said it."

"Well, what did he say?" Sally demanded.

"He said, 'Where's Dave? Now it's a pea-soup fog, your friend ought to be out doing a little extra hauling for himself.' "

David was relieved. "He was only kidding, Poke. The men do a lot of teasing. Willis knows I wouldn't go haul in a fog like this."

"Probably." Poke brightened as they approached the foursquare colonial building that housed Saturday Cove's Historical Society, and the incident was quickly forgotten.

Sally's spirits were high. Elated, she jumped the cracks in the sidewalk. "Just think," she whispered with a superior glance at the passers-by, "we're about to go hunting for a buried treasure, and not a soul in town knows it."

"Except Roddie McNeill," David reminded her.

"And Uncle Charlie," Poke added in the interests of accuracy.

Together, they entered the dim hall. Mira Piper, the custodian, glanced up from her desk. Her welcome was so genuine that Poke gave her one of his rare, warm smiles.

"We're looking for material on the Revolutionary history of Saturday Cove," he explained.

"Wonderful, Elijah!" The little woman nodded appreciatively. "I love to see our young people take an interest in the town history. Now you and Sally and David just follow me." Like a sparrow she fluttered ahead of them into a reading room. Darting in and out among the files, she soon had the long table piled with volumes and records.

63

"We'll take good care of everything, Miss Piper," David promised.

"And our hands are nice and clean," Sally put in.

Mira Piper laughed. "I'd already glanced at them," she confessed. "I've always trusted children with these precious old things," she told them, "and I've never once been disappointed. When you're through looking at them just leave them on this table. I'll put them away." Then, with a quick nod, away flew Mira Piper, back to her desk, leaving behind her a delicate fragrance of roses.

All three of them sniffed contentedly for a moment. Then they settled down to work, each with a heavy book. For some time there was silence.

"Aha!" said Poke suddenly.

Sally and David looked up. "What?" they asked, both at once.

"It says here," whispered Poke earnestly, "that masses of soft limestone can be found in this area along with the more common red sandstone and greenstone and granite."

"Oh, for heaven's sake, Poke," David broke in. "What are you reading?"

Poke looked seriously at the cover. "*Lithographs of the Penobscot Bay Area,*" he read.

"What does that have to do with the Blake treasure?"

"One never knows," rumbled Poke. "Interesting fact, though, isn't it?" Greedily, he resumed his reading.

David, with a tolerant shake of his head, returned to the mass of material piled in front of them.

The long minutes ticked loudly past. Sally read on

64

about the early days of Saturday Cove — its first settlement by John Blake on the island at the head of the inlet, the cutting of timber on the mainland, the visits of the Indians who were peaceful during this period, the slow growth of the village along its present Main Street.

Outside, the foghorn moaned without ceasing. On Blake's Island the fog would be swirling up the path and about the old house. Again, by the flickering glimmer of the candle, she seemed to see Jonathan's faded chart. Sharply, she smelled again the cold dampness of the buttery and felt the shadows of the ages reaching out of the silence.

Softly closing her book, Sally tiptoed away from the table and inspected the case of Indian and colonial relics that stood against the wall. Arrowheads. Grapeshot. Militia buttons. Her eyes fell on one button, dull and flat and as large as a silver dollar. A card beneath it bore the legend, "Pewter. Revolutionary War Period. Rare. Found on Blake's Island." Sally stared at it, reflecting that it might long ago have graced the coat of John Blake, American patriot. Then, impatiently, she hurried back to the table. David's sunburned face and Poke's pale one were still bent in identical attitudes. David had just started on the contents of a manila envelope filled with faded papers.

"This might take days," Sally told herself. Discouraged, she sat down again and leafed through another book.

Then David whispered, "Poke! Sally! I think I've found something." For a moment he gazed at the paper he held in his hand. Then he glanced up at them. "This is a letter written in 1779 by John Blake to a relative living in Salem."

"Oh, read it!" cried Sally, and Poke leaned forward with interest.

David cleared his throat. "Dear Joel, Our regiment, which was let go home for the mowing, is again to be mustered and I am to leave this day. I beg of you, Cousin, will you remember that my good wife, Sally, and our children must fend alone for themselves on this island whilst I am gone, and that if the worst should happen to me, I pray that you, my kinfolk, will have a thought for them."

Sally caught her breath. "Oh, poor John Blake."

"He came back safely," David reminded her. "Now listen to this, We are free men fighting on free soil to hold what we have against tyranny. I have faith that I shall return right soon to see to the harvest, and to another important matter. . . ."

"I wonder . . . ." Poke mused.

"Yet again last night we had considerable trouble from the raiders."

"This is it!" Poke broke in.

"They were off a British frigate of about fifty tons which before sunset came in with the tide. Several of these robbers laid hold on me as I was employed in the barn. They shot my oxen and killed two of my lambs which they quartered and carried aboard their barge. Others of the company entered my house and brought away two muskets of great value."

"They lived by their muskets then," Poke broke in.

66

". . . two firkins of butter, and the roast of venison made ready for the evening meal. They would likewise have plundered the house of other articles of value, but that my brave Sally caused these to be taken away to a place of safety by our son, Jonathan.

"This very night there came up a wind of such force that we were soon rid of the Lobster-backs and did much rejoice in the safe return after two hours of our eldest son. . . ."

David laid down the letter and looked up, his eyes shining.

Poke released a long breath. "Question: How long was Jonathan gone? Answer: Two hours. Question: Where did he go? Answer: To whichever island he could reach and return from in that time."

"Bucking a head wind one way," David reminded them.

"And with time out to hide the treasure," Poke added.

But Sally was not satisfied. "If all this is true, then I don't see why they didn't go back later on, after the British left, and dig the treasure up again."

"Something happened," Poke stated. "Something that made recovering it right away impossible. John Blake certainly intended to unearth it when he got home from his regiment. Remember, he wrote, I shall return right soon to see to the harvest, *and to another important matter*. But something had happened, and neither John Blake nor his son, Jonathan, ever recovered the valuables."

Sally was downcast. "I know what happened," she said gloomily. "Somebody else dug them up before

Jonathan and his father went back for them. That's what happened."

David shook his head. "In that case they would have found an empty hole when they went to dig. Then the family story wouldn't have come down to us the way it did. It would have been the story of a stolen treasure, not a lost one."

"Could they possibly have forgotten where it was hidden?" Poke then asked.

David thought for a moment. "If they had, wouldn't that have been part of the story? We never heard that they did any hunting for the treasure, though folks have hunted plenty since then."

Poke nodded slowly. "That's right. But for some reason they couldn't recover it, either before John Blake went away or after he returned. And yet, they kept the hiding place secret, so they must have expected to get the things again sometime."

Sally, not altogether understanding, looked from one of the boys to the other, content to let them do the reasoning. The old story had begun to come to life. It was taking misty shape from facts long hidden.

Eagerly, David took up the narrative. "If they didn't recover the treasure in their lifetimes, then the valuables have stayed right where Jonathan hid them the night the British came."

"But why didn't Jonathan pass on the secret to his children?" Sally demanded.

"I'll bet he meant to," David said softly. "Dad once told me that Jonathan went down with one of his own ships off the coast of Africa while he was still quite young. So perhaps the only clue he ever left was the chart he drew when he was a boy."

"Only clue," Poke shook his head. "This case is packed with clues. John's letter to his relative in Salem tells us how long Jonathan was gone. That, in turn, will tell us which of the islands he rowed to. We know that Jonathan and his father waited their lifetimes for something to happen in order to recover their treasure. And we know that they never recovered it. Something must have happened to the hiding place." He looked to his friends for help but, carried along on Poke's enthusiasm, they had nothing new to offer. "If we hunt with our minds are well as our eyes," he told them, "we may find it. . . ."

Sally leaped to her feet. "Come on! Let's go out to Blake's this very minute and start rowing."

"When you find the island that lies about an hour's row from Blake's," said Poke, "you'll have your treasure."

But they went outside into a fog that was, if anything, thicker than ever.

"It's bound to clear tomorrow," said Poke, and Sally crossed her fingers.

But the next morning Saturday Cove was fogbound, and the town knew that it was in for a "spell of weather." For two more days the foghorn on Big Fox Island blew steadily. Automobiles, when they moved at all, crawled half-blind through Main Street with their headlights on. In the Cove the lobster boats lay motionless, at anchor.

"If it gets any thicker," said David in disgust, "the sea gulls will be walking."

At first David and Sally railed against the fog. Repeatedly, they peered through the windows to see if, in spite of the weather reports, the fog showed signs of lifting. Neither mentioned the McNeills, nor the deeds to Little Fox and Blueberry Islands. But each knew that the other thought of little else.

To take their minds off the passing of time, David did chores and projects that he never got around to doing in hauling weather, and Sally helped him. Together, they mended the chicken wire. They cleaned the barn. They put up a new tire swing in the loft.

And once each day David, in return, gave Sally a swimming lesson on the foggy beach at Goose Creek. But it was no use. The instant the cold water closed over Sally's head she scurried out and, to David's disgust, refused to go in again.

Occasionally Poke came over. Rather indifferently, the three of them did experiments with David's old chemistry set, or shot for baskets in the barn.

Finally, on the third long day the wind changed. The wind changed into the northeast only to blow up a gale that lashed at the coast in concentrated fury. Silent and defeated, David watched the rain stream blindingly against the windows, watched the elms toss in the wind, listened to the torrents of water gushing from the rainspouts outside. "This means there'll be plenty of repairs to make on the gear," he told Sally gloomily.

Then he brought out his twine. Together, he and Sally knitted heads for the lobster traps, thinly content with at least this much of the sea. And by late afternoon the storm had begun to spend itself.

Mrs. Blake said at supper, "This is a williwaw, all right, a real old-fashioned northeaster. But it will begin to move out tomorrow. You'll see."

And she was right.

The next morning Sally ran into David's room. "You

can see all the way to the road," she cried. "It's still foggy, but you can make out the tulip tree as clear as anything."

"Then let's go!" said David. He was eager to tend to his neglected traps, to check his gear for damage done by the storm. But his interest in the Blake treasure had, like Sally's, mounted with the delay. The traps could wait, as usual, until the afternoon.

Soon after breakfast they were on their way. Fog still shrouded Saturday Cove, but it no longer seemed like a solid wall. Rather, the mist was in motion, swirling and thinning to show weird glimpses of familiar things.

It was good to be in action again. Sally trotted along in silence for a while beside her brother. Then she lifted her head and sang:

"Cape Cod boys they have no sleds,
Heave away! Heave away — !"

And David joined in:

"They slide down dunes on codfish heads,
We are bound for Califor-ni-ay!"

When they reached Harbor Road they met Mira Piper just leaving her little house at the top of the hill.

"Well," she smiled at them, "aren't we all up bright and early. Just like Noah's animals coming out of the ark after their spell of weather." She walked along beside them, chatting as rapidly as she walked.

She twitters just like a happy robin, thought Sally, liking her.

"Tell me," said Mira Piper, "do you two young people know the McNeill boy?"

"Not very well, Miss Piper," said David.

"Not nearly so well as we'd like to," Sally added wickedly. David nudged her.

"Such a quiet boy. So interested in history. He was in to see me the very day you were. Just think of it, David and Sally," she smiled, "new to town, and already taking an interest in our history."

"Think of that!" Sally said to David with special meaning.

"But so lonely," Mira Piper went on. "Perhaps you two and that nice Elijah Stokes could make friends with the poor boy."

"Perhaps we could," said Sally, so sweetly that she received another nudge from her brother.

Then David said quickly, "Miss Piper, did you show Roddie the same old records that you got out for us?"

"Oh, yes. The town history is available to everyone, you know." They had reached the Historical Society building and Mira Piper paused dreamily in the doorway. "Just think, children. This old house was new at the very same time that the British raided Blake's Island." She gave them a bright smile. "Come in again soon and bring the McNeill boy with you. He's so interested in history, and he seems so lonely." Then she disappeared inside, hopeful that she had sown the seeds of friendship between the Blake children and Roddie McNeill.

74

When they were beyond hearing Sally sputtered, "So lonely! And *so* interested in the Blake treasure!"

"We don't really know Roddie," said David. "Maybe he just likes history."

Sally's voice was flat. "We know him well enough. We know he likes to show off in boats. And we know he likes to spy on people."

David grinned. "If you hadn't been spying, yourself, we'd never have known that."

"Well, that proves he has our chart, or he would never have bothered to spy on us." Sally brightened. "Why don't we just ask him for it?"

David laughed shortly. "Roddie," he said, pretending a conversation, "if it isn't too much to ask, would you be so kind as to hand over our chart? Look, Sally, if he found it and kept it in the first place, he wouldn't give it up now, would he? Especially since he has found out that there really was a treasure."

Sally shook her head.

"Let's say he does have the chart. He's boned up on town history as well. His dad has bought a couple of the islands in question. Well, then, he probably figures it's every man for himself, and the winner take all."

"That's what Mr. McNeill was saying at Uncle Charlie's antique shop," Sally remembered. "And he said that a smart operator finds the short cuts or he gets left."

Unconsciously, they began to walk faster. They reached the docks just as Perce Dennett drove his bait truck out onto Main Street. David raised his hand in greeting, but the man seemed not to see him.

75

"It's a good thing this is bait day," David told Sally. "I was just about flat out of redfish."

"I wish you didn't have to haul this afternoon," Sally complained, not interested in the redfish. "I wish we could row all day."

"We'll do what we have time for."

"If only Poke would go out in a boat," said Sally with a flash of her old resentment. "Then he and I could row out to all the islands while you're hauling."

David agreed with her, but remained silent.

"If only Mother didn't mind if I rowed alone."

"You have to learn to swim, first," David reminded her.

Sally, downcast, said no more.

They stopped at the gear shed only long enough to get the oars. As they passed the bait barrel, David stopped, surprised. "That's funny. Perce didn't leave me any bait."

He looked into the barrels grouped by the other shacks. Each was filled to the brim with briney, salted redfish.

"He must have forgotten you," said Sally.

"He never did before." Frowning, David followed Sally down the ramp.

Back in the dory again, the motor taking life under his hands, he decided that it didn't matter if Perce had forgotten him. Willis Greenlaw or Foggy Dennett would lend him enough bait for the day.

The *Lobster Boy* swung slowly into the cove. A short way out they caught sight of a figure sculling his skiff slowly in toward Fishermen's Dock.

"There's Willis coming in from hauling," said David
with relief. He cut back the motor and greeted the
lobsterman. "Could you let me have a little bait later
on?" he called. "I'm flat out and Perce forgot to leave
me any."

His words hung unanswered on the fog. Without
changing expression, Willis Greenlaw continued steadily on his way.

Silently, they stared after him.

Sally said in a puzzled voice, "Maybe he didn't hear
you."

But David was remembering that Willis had approached Poke in the drugstore a few days before.
What was it he had said? "Now it's a pea-soup fog,

your friend, Dave Blake, ought to be out doing a little extra hauling for himself."

"But what are they worrying about?" David asked himself. "Even if I did haul in a pea-souper, even if I got lost, it wouldn't hurt them any."

David glanced at Sally's anxious face and forced a smile. "Maybe it wasn't Willis, after all. It's hard to see in this fog." But it was Willis, all right. David had seen him clearly when the mist had thinned for a moment. A dark worry began to nag at him.

Then they were *put-putting* into the fog. Maybe Willis hadn't heard him. Or maybe his mind had been on something else. David forced his attention back to the task of guiding the dory out of the cove.

"We'll use the motor as far as Blake's," David shouted. "Then we'll start rowing to Little Fox. Then Blueberry. Because if the McNeills don't own those islands yet, they soon will."

Close to the shore of Blake's, David shut off the motor and checked his watch. "If Little Fox is the right island, we should be there in less than an hour. That would give Jonathan time to hide the things and row back against a head wind."

David headed the dory for the bell buoy that would serve as a bearing on Little Fox Island beyond. Neither spoke as he pulled easily, steadily at the oars. But both of them had the same thought, Was this the course that young Jonathan had taken, alone and in danger, that windy night so long ago?

Soon the dismal *clang, clang,* of the buoy grew louder. The red marker became visible beside them, rising and falling on the long swells. Then, very gradually, the outline of Little Fox Island took form beyond the buoy.

Now and then as they rowed on, the muffled sound of a motor came to them and a lobster boat moved into their view and out again. But otherwise this was an unearthly trip. It seemed to David that they were alone in a wet, white world where everyday things did not exist.

When they turned into the sheltered cove of the island, David looked at his watch. "Forty minutes. Sally, Jonathan could have come to Little Fox. He could have hidden the treasure here."

But Sally did not answer. She sat frozen in the bow, staring at something just beyond.

Not ten yards away lay the *Pirate*, Roddie McNeill's boat, her narrow hull gleaming against the gray water.

Then, through the fog, they heard the sounds of a spade striking into rocky island soil.

Chapter

6

DISCOVERY AND DISASTER

DAVID felt the hot flood of anger rise within him. By hook and by crook, by keeping their chart and by spying on them, Roddie had taken the short cuts and gotten there first.

"What shall we do?" Sally whispered.

David listened. The sounds of the spade stopped. He studied the woods beyond the ledge.

"It looks as if we won't have to do anything," he said shortly.

For a figure had appeared at the edge of the spruces and now swung down the path toward them. It was Roddie McNeill, and he was carrying a spade. From the height of the ledge he looked them over coolly. "Sorry. This is private property."

Indignantly, Sally cried out, "This is Blake land! It always has been." But her voice sounded all at once unsure, and Roddie smiled.

"Not any more it isn't. My father has just passed papers on Little Fox. Also, my friends, on Blueberry Island."

David's knuckles whitened at the handles of the oars, but he forced himself to speak levelly. "McNeill land, maybe. But it's Blake treasure you're digging for."

"Blake treasure? You don't say!" Roddie's smile was insolent. "It just happens that buried treasure belongs to the person who finds it. Ask any good lawyer — if there is such a thing in Saturday Cove," he added with scorn.

For a moment there was silence and the *Lobster Boy* rocked on the little waves that lapped on the beach.

Then Sally's voice rose despairingly. "We lost our treasure chart, and I bet anything you found it. And that's just plain stealing, no matter what you say!"

Roddie lifted his brows. "So you lost some chart. What makes you think I have it?"

"Because anybody else in our town would have given it back," Sally answered hotly.

For an instant Roddie hesitated. Then he shrugged. "If you two know so much, why don't you come ashore and look around? Nothing can happen to you. Except that when I get back to town I'll have you both arrested for trespassing, that's all."

Sally's chin quivered with fury. "But what about the treasure?" she wailed. "It's ours!"

With an unsteady hand, David reached out to keep the old dory from drifting against the gleaming hull of the *Pirate*. There was nothing to say.

Roddie smiled, sure of himself again. "From what I can see of the Blakes, I doubt if they ever had any treasure to hide." He dipped his spade at them. "See you around, I'm afraid." And he turned back into the fog.

Then there was nothing but the empty ledge and the dim path, and the fine mist raining down onto their upturned faces.

Sally's mouth quivered and a tear moved down one cheek.

"Let's get out of here," David muttered. "Roddie's won the first round. But that doesn't mean he'll win the second." Grimly, he started up the motor and they began the return trip in silence.

"David? What about Blueberry Island?" Sally asked finally.

"I guess Blueberry and Little Fox are about the same distance from Blake's. So Jonathan could have rowed to one as well as the other. But since we can't go ashore on either of them, we're no better off now than we were before." David's voice trailed away. "Maybe we'd just better forget the treasure, Sally. I'll be pretty busy with the new traps, anyway."

But Sally clung to the subject. "What about Big Fox, then?"

David glanced at the clearing shape of the island that lay farthest from Blake's. From its seaward point still came the slow blast of the foghorn. He shook his head. "We can save ourselves the row, Sally. Big Fox is too far. If Jonathan had gone out there, it would have taken him longer than two hours out and back, especially with a wind coming up." David looked away, as if he were through with the subject.

But Sally searched the cove with speculative eyes. Where would a boy row if he wanted to hide something? She gazed at The Graves, scattered bare ledges rising out of the sea, and beyond those at The Cobbles, half hidden in the fog. There were so many of them — mountain tops with all except their granite skulls drowned in the sea. Were they ledge or island, Sally wondered.

Curiously, David followed her gaze. "I don't think Jonathan would have headed out there. I've been ashore on most of them and they're solid ledge. Besides, they're too exposed. He could have been seen too easily."

But although Sally's shoulders still drooped, her heart lifted. David was no longer ready to forget about the treasure. He was thinking again.

They had left the bell buoy tossing in their wake. David was squinting toward Blake's Island and little Tub. Perhaps, he mused, it would be a good idea to set the last of the new traps between the two islands. Then a thought came to him that sent shivers along his arms. Surprised, he stared at Sally. "Tub Island!" he cried. "We never once thought of little Tub Island. We're so used to walking to it over the bar from Blake's, we forgot that at high tide it's a separate island. Sally, there's a fifty-fifty chance the tide was full that night, and it was *Tub* that Jonathan rowed to!"

Excited, Sally leaned forward. "How can we find out? From some ship's log, maybe?"

David's spirits like Sally's had risen high. But now they sank again and David shook his head. "They didn't generally log the tides, just wind direction and

84

weather. I don't see how we can ever find out about a tide that long ago."

The *Lobster Boy* pulsed slowly through the gray-bright morning, and Sally began to wonder. If only she could reason how the tide was running the night the British came, then she might make up to David for losing the old chart. . . .

Suddenly she remembered something. "David! The letter!"

Her brother looked at her blankly.

"John Blake's letter! He wrote about the raiders coming ashore off a frigid."

David laughed. "A frigate."

"A frigate, then," Sally said impatiently, "that came in *with the tide* before sunset! And the British must have gone straight ashore at Blake's because they stole the roast that Sally was cooking for supper, remember?"

"I'll say I do!" David's voice grew strong. "Then the tide was coming in! When Jonathan left with the valuables, it must have been close to flood tide. So it could have been Tub that he rowed to that night."

Sally said nothing, but she felt warmed and happy.

"And Sally! An enemy ship would lie off Blueberry Island, out where she would be hidden from the village, wouldn't she? Now, if you were Jonathan and didn't want the British to see you, where would you *not* head?"

Sally thought. "I wouldn't head out toward either of the Fox Islands, or Blueberry, or any of the ledges," she said slowly, "and I wouldn't head in toward town. Because either way I might be seen by the frigid."

"Frigate," said David automatically. "So?"

"So I'd sneak off the back shore of Blake's and keep in close to the ledges. I'd stay behind Blake's wherever I could, and then they wouldn't see me, either the men on the frigate or those who came ashore at the front cove. Then I'd head . . . ." Sally stopped and stared at David, her eyes widening.

"You'd head for Tub Island, Sally," David's voice rose with excitement, "because there's no better place to go."

Sally nodded, then fiercely she hugged her knees. "Just let Roddie McNeill dig! Let him keep his old islands! Oh, David, let's go to Tub and hunt for the treasure this very minute!"

David shook his head. "We can plan on plenty of digging before we turn up that treasure. Besides, I want to hear what Poke has to say about this. Maybe . . . ."

"Maybe he'll even come, too." Sally finished his thought. "Oh, David, now that we're getting warm, maybe Poke will even come out in the dory with us."

David nodded slowly. "Maybe." He looked at his watch. "Let's go home to lunch. Then, if I get through hauling in time, we might even start digging on Tub today. It'll take a while, you know, even if Poke does come and help." He cut back his speed and guided the dory down the long thoroughfare of the inner harbor.

"I don't care," Sally said carelessly. "I don't care if it takes a week. I have a feeling something big is going to happen."

Poke was washing windows at the Harbor Supply. Gravely, he tossed them each a cleaning cloth. "Don't tell me," he said as he scanned their faces. "I can guess. You have discovered the island where Jonathan hid the valuables."

David grinned at his friend and set to work beside him. "See what you think." Then, with frequent additions from Sally, he told Poke about the quarrel with Roddie on Little Fox Island, and about Sally's remembering that the tide was coming in on the night of the island raid on Blake's. "And besides," David finished, "Tub is the only island Jonathan could be sure of reaching without being spotted by the British. Blake's would have hidden him all the way."

Poke shook his head in generous admiration. "Why didn't I figure that out before?"

"Why didn't I? I've wondered about all this longer than you have."

"From now on," Poke announced, "Sally can be chief adviser of all our treasure hunts."

Sally squirmed with pleasure and gave her window an extra hard polish. There beyond Grindstone Point lay Tub Island, a small circle separated from Blake's by the full tide.

"It looks like a pie with a bite taken out of it," she mused.

"That 'bite,' " Poke rumbled in his lecture voice, "is probably due to the wind and wave erosion of a mass of soft limestone like I read to you about from the lithograph book. Why, do you realize that the granite around here is tunneled through and through?"

"Sure, Poke," David interrupted cheerfully. "I'm sorry, but we've got to get going. What we really came in for was, well, to ask you to come out to Tub Island with us later on . . . ." His voice trailed away at the strange expression in the older boy's dark eyes.

"This looks like trouble coming," said Poke quietly, looking out the window.

Across the wharf toward the Supply came several of the lobstermen, walking heavily, their faces somber.

Unexpectedly, the dark thought shot again like a quick pain into David's mind. This time he faced it. Something was terribly wrong between him and the men.

He was aware of his heart pounding in his ears like a warning drum. Quick pictures flashed before his mind — Willis Greenlaw saying, "Now it's a pea-soup fog, your friend ought to be out doing a little extra

hauling . . . ." And Perce Dennett, turning away from David as he drove the truck up from the docks. The bait barrel standing empty beside the shed. Willis sculling across the cove, pretending not to see him.

Now he would at least learn what the trouble was. The boy thrust his fists tightly into his pockets and faced them, waiting.

Slowly, they filed into the store, Willis Greenlaw first and behind him Foggy Dennett, then his brother, Perce, and the others. Mostly they avoided David's eyes and remained silent. But Willis cleared his throat, and with his gaze steady on David he spoke to the older boy. "Poke, my boat's down to the float. Fill her up, will you?"

Reluctantly, Poke went outside to the gas pumps.

"Well, Dave. You want Sally to hear this?" Willis began, not unkindly.

The sick uneasiness grew inside David, but he replied steadily enough, "Sally can hear anything you want to say, Willis."

Willis drew a heavy breath. "Someone's hauling our traps, Dave. Every single one of us here and a couple that aren't back in yet, we're all being hauled. Have been for a couple weeks now."

David stared at him. Why, hauling another man's traps was the final crime among lobstermen.

"We know none of us full-timers is doing it," Willis continued. "We've made a living hauling together since we was your age, and we don't aim to start cheating on each other now. But, well . . . ." Willis walked a few paces down the store, then he turned and came back. "Some of us thought that maybe a kid might not see it that way, 'specially if he was just hauling part-time for extra money."

Sally caught her breath sharply, and David dug his nails into his palms and fought for control. He was waiting for Willis to say it. Why didn't he come right out and say it?

But Willis shrugged and glanced at Foggy Dennett.

"Well, David, speak up!" Foggy sounded surprised and miserable. "You tell us your side of it. Maybe things aren't as bad as they look." Foggy was asking him to deny it.

Now, now was the time to tell them that he had never hauled another man's traps in his life, and that he never intended to! But, to David's horror, the tears pricked hotly behind his eyelids and his throat began to fill. He could not trust himself to speak.

"Maybe you're wondering how we found out." Willis struck a match and held it to his pipe. "Well, the bait line knotted different, usually. And sometimes the button not shut on the door. And no lobsters, time and time again, and no bait, either, for two, three weeks now."

Perce Dennett spoke up. "Those traps are prob'ly being hauled late in the day after the rest of us have got back in."

For a moment no one said anything, then Foggy added sadly, "You're the only one of us that hauls late, Dave. And your catch hasn't slacked off any. Willis checked, over to the hotel."

"Lately, you're out more often, too, some of us have noticed," said Perce.

But I've been putting down extra traps, pleaded David silently. And I've been hauling steady to meet the taxes on Blake's. I've even been fooling around the cove hunting for treasure.

But the words remained unspoken behind the shameful ache in his throat.

Willis shook his head. "We know you got a good reason to make extra money, what with saving up for your education. But that sort of hauling's no good, son. No good at all."

David looked at these men whose rough hands had taught him the work he loved. All his life he had cherished their respect. To stand before them now as a lobster thief was nightmarish. He pressed his lips tightly together to hide their trembling.

"You won't talk?" Willis asked gently.

David drew an unsteady breath. He must speak up now, or it would be too late.

Poke came in and Willis absently counted out the money. Without looking at David he said, "I wish this needn't have happened."

Foggy turned to go. He looked very tired. "We've been talkin' this over the past three days, Dave. Perce won't sell you any more bait. You better quit haulin' for a while. We'll see if our catch picks up any."

Then the men filed out, slowly, as they had come.

David, staring after them, saw his bright world dissolve into ugliness. *David Blake, lobster thief.*

The west wind, rising, tore great shreds out of the fog and flung them across the cove. Blindly, David turned and headed for home. Sally moved to follow him, but Poke held her back.

"Let him go," he said softly. "He wants to be alone."

When the door closed behind David, Poke burst into a rare scorn. "Stealing lobsters? David? What a brilliant idea!" He brought his fist down hard against the counter.

"He didn't even deny it, Poke." Sally's eyes began to fill with tears. "He didn't even speak up."

"He couldn't," said Poke.

"They said David's the only one who hauls late, and he's the only one who hasn't lost any of his catch."

Poke frowned out at the bay.

"They'll keep him from hauling," cried Sally un-evenly. "But let them! Just let them! Then they'll see it's somebody else who is stealing their old lobsters."

Poke shook his head. "If David doesn't go out for a while, I have an idea that the real thief will just lie low, too. Otherwise, he would have been hauling Dave's traps right along with the others. As I see it, somebody is hoping to get away with stealing by letting David take the blame. Then when Dave starts hauling again, so does the thief. A nice piece of work!"

"But why don't the men see it that way?"

"Because everything points to David, and they think they don't need to look any farther. This is nothing sudden, Sally," Poke added thoughtfully. "There have been little signs of trouble, if we had known enough to understand them. From Lookout Rock we watched Foggy hauling the other day. He spent a long time with one trap. David thought it was because of a full catch, but probably he was studying the knots in his bait line and wondering if someone had been hauling him."

"Well, I bet it's that old Willis Greenlaw! He's mean to talk to David the way he did. And David just stood there and — and looked at him and didn't say a word." Loud grief burst over Sally. Silently, Poke handed her his handkerchief.

"They'll take his license away from him, Poke," Sally sobbed. "And his license means more to him than anything in the world."

"No, Sally, they won't," Poke said gently, "because they haven't any real proof. David can't lose his license unless the warden catches him in the act of hauling illegally. I don't think they want to call in the warden. Not yet, anyway." The boy put an awkward hand on Sally's shoulder.

After a while she blew her nose and looked up at Poke with reddened eyes. "But David can't haul without bait, Poke."

"How about herring?"

Sally shook her head miserably. "The Dennetts know everybody who does any seining. If they won't sell him any redfish, they'll keep him from getting herring, too."

Something darkened in Poke's eyes. "Will it matter so much if David doesn't go out hauling for a while?"

"Matter!" cried Sally. "If he stops hauling now he'll miss the peak season. He'll lose Blake's Island because he won't have any money to pay the taxes."

Poke's deep voice was suddenly very firm. "Then he'll just have to keep on hauling."

Sally nodded doubtfully, but a tiny light of hope had come into her face. "We could go fishing maybe, for pollack or mackerel. Off the wharf, I mean," she added hastily. "I don't mean in a boat."

Poke smiled crookedly. "I know what you mean, Sally. But I'm afraid Dave will need more bait than we could catch on a line."

Sally looked down, defeated.

"I'll find a way," said Poke. "Now you run along home and let me think."

Sally ran. She ran until she reached Harbor Road, but her brother was nowhere in sight. Out of breath

and discouraged, she slowed to a walk. Her feet felt
heavy and her heart was like lead. If she thought about
what had just happened she would surely start to cry
again. So she picked a daisy in passing and thought
instead about the treasure.

"Rich man, poor man, beggarman, thief . . ." Sally
said to herself as she counted off the petals.

Somehow she knew that David would not take her
to Tub Island right away. If he couldn't get bait, he
might keep off the water altogether because of the
lobstermen. And if he could, the peak season for the
next few weeks would keep him too busy for treasure
hunting.

"Doctor, lawyer, Indian chief . . ." muttered Sally.
And Poke would never get into a boat, not for the
biggest treasure in the world. She knew that now. She
would have to go to Tub Island all by herself. But
how? Until she learned to swim, she would not be
allowed to take the dory out alone. Sally studied the
cove in despair.

At the rim of the harbor, the roof and chimneys of
the old house rose above the spruces on Blake's Island.

And behind Blake's lay little Tub, small and round,
like a secret.

"Tinker, tailor, soldier, sailor . . ." Slowly, Sally
walked homeward, her head bent over the daisy. She
would have to think of some way to get to Tub Island.

Chapter

7

EBB TIDE FOR DAVID

DISCONSOLATELY, David turned in at the front gate and looked up to see the familiar, ancient Ford parked in the driveway. Of course. Uncle Charlie had come. Now things would somehow straighten out — everything would be all right again. His heart lifted and he hurried into the house.

The old man was seated at the kitchen table with David's father and mother. Carefully, he set his coffee cup in its saucer and turned to face the boy. Uncle Charlie looked unhappy.

"David," he began, and his voice filled the room. "I been talking with your folks so's we can decide what you best do."

David glanced toward his mother. She seemed disturbed, but her smile was steady. Her look was filled with understanding.

"Stand over by the stove, David, and get warm. You look cold and damp." His father's voice, like his mother's smile, was reassuring.

David stood in front of the kitchen stove, feeling the good warmth at his back like a steadying arm.

Uncle Charlie cleared his throat and began loudly. "The boys over to the dock have been missing some lobsters, Dave."

"They told me, Uncle Charlie," said David. He was surprised that his voice did not shake.

"They say any more?"

"Yes." He met the old man's eyes steadily. "They asked me not to haul any more."

Now the explosion would come. Now Uncle Charlie's tremendous wrath would fall like a hurricane, whirling this nightmare up and away, destroying it for the evil thing it was.

David waited. The old clock on the mantel began to tick with an unbearable zest. TICK-*tock*, TICK-*tock*, TICK-*tock*. Still, Uncle Charlie stared into his coffee cup and said nothing.

Finally he sighed. "Well, Dave. They figure you're young and mebbe don't realize what's what. And you got a good reason, they think, to want some extry cash." Uncle Charlie slapped his chair in confusion. "Gorry mighty, Dave, they can't figure out why you haven't taken a loss yourself!"

"Unless I did it, you mean."

"Ayuh. That's about the jist of it." Uncle Charlie pushed back his chair and stood up. "And another thing. They figure those traps are gitting hauled late in the day after they're back in. Things are mostly the way they look, you know, and you're the only one goes out afternoons, Dave. They can't help wonderin'."

Then, with a shock, David understood. Uncle

Charlie, who should have trusted him, was one of those who wondered.

Mr. Blake met his son's look steadily. Buck up, he seemed to say. Tell him you didn't do it. That's what he wants to hear.

Suddenly David felt himself taller than the old man. He turned back to him and spoke carefully, as he would speak to a child. "Uncle Charlie, I never hauled anybody's traps but my own and I never will. The men know the reason I haul afternoons is because I work at home in the morning."

Embarrassed, Uncle Charlie looked away. But there was no mistaking the relief in his voice. "Shooty, Dave," he boomed, "I know it wa'n't you. But it's good to hear you say it, all the same."

David nodded.

"Now, look. Here's what you better do. You lay off haulin' for a while. Then they'll see it isn't you and they'll go after somebody else."

"Supposing the thief lays off, too?" David's father asked mildly.

"Well, I s'pose he might, during the peak season while the pickin's good. But give him time."

David found himself wondering if Uncle Charlie really believed there was someone else. "I guess maybe it would be easier to quit for a while," he said, thinking aloud.

" 'Course it is!" Uncle Charlie shouted. "When you see trouble coming, head the other way. Keep it to wind'ard, that's what I say. You'll live longer."

Why, grown men, even the finest of them, were not

98

always right, David thought with some surprise. Face up to trouble when it came. That was what his father always said, and in this case surely it was the thing to do. He lifted his head.

"I'm going hauling tomorrow, the way I always do. If I quit now the men will always believe I'm the thief. I'm going to keep right on hauling, Uncle Charlie. And if they call in the warden I'll be glad to take him along."

"Good for you," said David's father quietly, and although his mother was smiling there were proud tears in her eyes.

But Uncle Charlie shook his head as he rose to go.

"Thanks for the mug-up," he said to Mrs. Blake. Then he turned to David. "What are you going to do for bait?"

"I don't know," said David honestly.

"If you can't git bait you can't keep haulin', Dave, and mebbe that'll be just as well. But if you can, then you better forget your chores and haul mornings. Then they can keep an eye on you and they won't be talking."

"They don't have to keep an eye on me, Uncle Charlie, so I'm going out when I always go. But if they think their traps are being hauled late in the day, then I'll keep a lookout for someone else who goes out late."

Uncle Charlie sighed. "Well, they can't legally stop you unless they catch you stealing. But if you keep on haulin', they ain't a-going to like it." He managed a crooked smile by way of farewell and climbed wearily into his old car.

But David did not see him. Instead, he was seeing Roddie McNeill heading out of a cove that glowed red with the sunset.

David's father put a hand on his son's shoulder. "What now?"

David turned. "I think I know who is hauling those traps, Dad. Only I need proof."

His father nodded. "Then go after it, son."

The following day dawned blue and hot, and the bay was crystal clear. After an early lunch David made ready to leave for town, and Sally followed him around like an anxious puppy. For the first time this summer, she had failed to go to the beach for her swimming lesson. And for once, David noted gratefully, she had not begged to go hauling with him.

"What will you ever do for bait?" she worried.

"I don't know. I'll haul today anyway, and maybe I'll get enough crabs in the traps to tide me over. I don't know . . . ." David shrugged and headed unsmiling down the path. He sensed that Sally stood at the door and watched him with concern dark in her eyes. She, too, knew that whatever crabs he might haul up would not begin to bait his entire string. With an effort he straightened his shoulders and kept on toward town.

Most of the townspeople seemed not to have heard the ugly rumor that David Blake was a lobster thief, and they greeted him as cordially as ever. But even on that first day there were some who passed him by, silently and with chill faces.

When he reached Fishermen's Dock a few of the men were already in from hauling and, quietly busy, were carring their catch or putting away their gear. If they noticed David they gave no sign.

He went on down the path to the gear shed and his heart was like a stone. He found himself remembering things that had meant so much — the friendly banter across the water when he passed them coming in, the exchange of news around the gear sheds, Foggy's special greeting, "Good haulin', pal!"

All right, David thought with a deep bitterness. His face could be as stony as theirs. He could match their silence with his own. Heavily, he flung open the door of the gear shed and paused, bewildered. The rich, wonderful smell of salt redfish rose strong among the pleasant odors of potwarp and spruce wood. David stared at his bait barrel, filled to the brim. A quick hope rose within him as he wondered which of the lobstermen still believed in his honesty.

Outside, steps crunched on the clamshell path and Poke peered in. His unruly hair was edged by sunlight. A smile lighted his face. "There's more where that came from," he said.

David hesitated. "How did you do it, Poke?"

"Simple," said Poke and he seated himself on the workbench. "I had a little talk with Mira Piper who agreed that lobster bait would make a fine fertilizer for her prize roses. So this morning Uncle Fred drove us to Rockland where we got a barrel of, uh, fertilizer from the bait company. It seems," added Poke with a wink, "that Uncle Fred is growing interested in roses and has taken to calling on Miss Piper to talk about them."

"Well, what do you know!" said David, interested.

Poke grinned in answer. "And furthermore, Miss Piper said to tell you that she has taken out what fertilizer she wants. You are to have the rest of it if she may store her barrel in your shed." And Poke surveyed the full barrel with a fond pride.

David's eyes began to sting, but laughter, too, crowded into his throat. He shook his head, unable to thank his friend properly. "I'll settle tomorrow, Poke, when the hotel pays me."

"That's all right." Then Poke hesitated, frowning down at the rough floor. "You asked me to be a partner on the *Lobster Boy*, but I think you know how I feel about boats."

David nodded, waiting.

"Well, how about counting me in as a sort of silent partner? You do the hauling and I'll supply the bait. Then we'll be in this thing together."

David's throat tightened at his friend's loyalty. The two shook hands on the agreement.

"One other thing. Don't let the men get you down," Poke urged. "All we have to do, you know, is find the real thief." Significantly he tapped the battered field glasses slung over one thin shoulder. "Whenever our friend Roddie McNeill roars away from the yacht club, I intend to be watching."

"But I never said I thought it was . . . ."

"You didn't have to," said the older boy. "Furthermore, I have generously offered to wait on tables at the yacht club dinner each Saturday. Young McNeill will be there, talking, I hope. And young Stokes will be there, too, listening." Poke winked and was gone.

With new courage David filled his bait can. Now he could keep Blake's Island and he could continue his savings program. And, by the grace of fortune, he could clear his name of dishonor.

When David went down to the dory carrying his bait can he walked with his head held high. But for all the notice given him by the lobstermen, he might never have been there at all.

That afternoon, and several times in the days to

104

follow, David found himself off Tub Island. But he put the thought of treasure impatiently from his mind. If it had not been for Jonathan's old chart and the merry chase it had led them, perhaps he would have seen trouble coming in time to prevent it. Certainly, until he had cleared his name, until he had met his obligation to Blake's Island and to his college fund, he had no time for treasure hunting. It seemed to David that he was growing up, overnight, that he was becoming a man, engaged in a man's livelihood filled with danger and competition. He thought often enough of Uncle Charlie's warning, "If you keep on haulin', they ain't a-going to like it."

As the hot, clear days went by, David began to understand what the old man had meant. Everyone was getting a good catch. Prices were high. The traps apparently had not been tampered with of late. But day after day more of the townspeople left him strictly alone. By the end of the following week it seemed to David that Saturday Cove, lobstermen and townspeople together, had shrunk to his own family and the few friends who had stood by him — Poke, Mira Piper, and Poke's Uncle Fred Kibbe at the Harbor Supply.

"The men are afraid of you," Poke told him one day as they sat mending trap heads on the doorstep of the shed. "They think that when lobsters get scarce they'll find their traps hauled again."

"Do they ever say anything about how I get my bait?" David asked him curiously.

"They make a remark now and then. But that sort of thing doesn't bother Uncle Fred. Whenever your bait gets low Mira Piper seems to need some more, uh, rose fertilizer."

David shifted restlessly on the doorstep. What right, after all, did he have to ask Fred Kibbe to befriend him? Soon the lobstermen might decide not to trade at the Supply.

"And Uncle Charlie always sticks up for you, too," Poke went on. "Lately, though, he hasn't been around very often."

Uncle Charlie isn't happy hanging around the dock any more, David thought, because he's ashamed. He taught me how to haul. And now that I have a bad record he thinks it's his fault. "Things are mostly the way they look," Uncle Charlie had said. And David Blake looked guilty.

"Poke," said David, suddenly desperate, "haven't you seen anything yet? With the field glasses, I mean."

The older boy shook his dark head. "How about you?"

"Whenever I haul," said David in a tight voice, "I keep one eye on any other boat in sight. There just hasn't been a thing wrong. No one even goes out of the cove late. Not regularly, anyway."

"I've been watching," said Poke, "and I've been asking questions. If Roddie is the thief, there is nothing to prove it now. He has set a few traps in shoal water off Grindstone Point, and some mornings he goes out early to tend them. But mostly he neglects them."

"Does he ever bring in more than a dozen pounds or so?"

Poke looked thoughtful. "I see what you mean. No,

no more than he could haul from his own traps. The men say," said Poke, "that Roddie knows very little about hauling and doesn't bother to learn. They tell him that that boat of his is getting as messy as an osprey's nest. But they seem to like him, and they don't question his honesty. Of course," said Poke, reaching for more twine, "he seems to have a good deal of spending money and he likes to treat. That helps, and it makes him feel like one of them, I suppose."

One of them, thought David with bitterness. "You don't ever see him heading out after I come back in? Around sunset or later?"

"From noon on, the *Pirate* lies off the yacht club as innocent as a lamb. Maybe," said Poke, "we're barking up the wrong tree."

David drew a heavy breath. "I'm beginning to think that getting proof I'm not guilty may take a long time, Poke."

"We can wait," said his friend quietly.

And wait they did through days grown short with the increased business of hauling. Twice each week David found a well-filled bait barrel in his shed. And bitter though he still felt at Perce's refusal to sell him bait, he could smile at the thought that it was Mira Piper, fragrant with the scent of roses, who was helping to supply him with the nose-twisting redfish. Somehow, the thought of Mira Piper and Poke and his Uncle Fred, drawn together on his behalf, made the lonely days more bearable.

One blazing Saturday noon David reached town on his bicycle a little earlier than usual. It was a "dog day," hot, David knew, even out on the bay. Already thirsty, he turned in at The Sandwich Shoppe near the dock for an orangeade. There in a fronth booth sat Roddie McNeill with Willis Greenlaw and the Dennetts. Seeing him, their conversation faltered. For a long moment David forced himself to meet the cool mockery of Roddie's stare.

"Hi, lobster boy," Roddie said softly.

Helpless, his face flaming, David sat down on a stool at the counter. Their dislike was a pillow held over his face, suffocating him. Then he heard Roddie's short laugh, and moments later they left the shop together, a closely knit and friendly group. Blindly, David reached for his orangeade. Without tasting it he had half emptied his glass when he heard a familiar voice beside him.

"Good morning, David. Aren't you the lucky one to be going out on the water on a hot day like this." Cheerfully, Mira Piper took the stool beside David and ordered an orangeade, too.

At once David began to feel better. He wished that he might tell this talkative little woman how grateful he was for what she had done to help him get his bait. "I want to say thank you," he began slowly.

"Dear me, you must mean for the rose fertilizer." Mira Piper's laugh trilled out delightedly. "I haven't had so much fun in years. I should thank *you* for letting me keep my fertilizer in your shed."

"You're welcome," said David with some confusion. "How are your roses doing?" he added politely.

"They're doing quite as well as your lobsters are," she declared. "Elijah and his Uncle Fred have kept me informed, David. I am very, very happy indeed that I can help a little."

They sipped their drinks in silence for a moment. Then the little woman turned to study David briefly. She appeared to make up her mind about something. "I have a problem, David, and I should like your opinion," she said briskly. "Do you remember that day when you came to the Society with Elijah and your sister, Sally?"

David nodded.

"And do you remember the glass case that holds the Revolutionary War relics? It stands in the reading room where you were," she reminded him.

"Yes, I remember."

"A button is missing, David, a very rare button." Her bright eyes searched his. "It is a pewter button from the field dress of a minuteman. My father found it years ago on Blake's Island and I myself had loaned it to the Society. Very likely it was the property of your ancestor, John Blake."

David felt the blood rise foolishly into his cheeks. Did Mira Piper imagine that he might have taken the button because it had once belonged to a Blake?

"Somebody," she went on clearly, "opened the case and took the button. It's valuable in itself, but as part of the history of Saturday Cove it is priceless. Whoever has taken it must care nothing about the town."

Roddie. Roddie McNeill had visited the Historical

Society that same day. Mira Piper herself had told them so. But what would Roddie want with an old button? David's thoughts whirled.

"I don't suppose," Mira went on, "that you have any idea of what might have become of it?"

David thought. Surely Roddie did not collect such things. And since, as Poke had said, he had plenty of spending money, he would not have stolen it to sell it. No, there was no reason to suppose that Roddie had taken the button, either to keep or to sell. David shook his head.

"No, I haven't any idea," he told her honestly.

"I see. Well, we shall just have to keep hoping that it will turn up," she told him. They finished their drinks companionably enough, but David felt ill at ease. Then, with a nod, Mira Piper was out of the shop and off down the street. Through the window he caught a swift glimpse of her face, friendly as ever, but thoughtful now, and troubled.

Would there never be an end to problems? He would ask Poke and Sally about the missing button, of course. But he knew that their mystification would equal his own.

Feeling hotter than before he had entered, David left the shop. The noon sun beat down upon Fishermen's Dock and glanced in waves off the cars parked near the warehouse. The chairs in front of the Supply, David noted with relief, were empty. There would be no lowered voices behind his back today.

With the sense of escaping a world that had grown too small, too harsh, David went off to haul, guiding the *Lobster Boy* steadily out of the harbor. The thwart felt blistering to his touch and the cove glared like copper. David raised his burning face, waiting to feel the first breeze off Grindstone Point. But today the air was still. Lifting the surface of the bay came the long, slow swells that told of storm winds raging somewhere south of them. "There'll be a good blow by night," David told himself.

He worked fast in spite of the heat, pausing now and then to dash the chill water over his face and arms and chest. As the afternoon lengthened the air grew more breathless.

A pleasure craft not unlike the *Pirate* passed close by. "Looks like we're in for it," called its skipper cheerfully.

"That ought to cool it off," David told him, grateful for the man's friendliness.

But although a few of the lobstermen neared him occasionally, hauling extra hours as they were during the peak season, there was no greeting from them, not the slightest sign of recognition. At the end of that sweltering afternoon, David felt depressed and weary as never before in his life. His affairs seemed to have reached a low ebb, and there was no sign that the tide would ever turn.

After supper he sat with his father on the lawn. Together, they watched the distant thunderheads roil up out of the south. "I feel as if I didn't have a friend in the world," David told him.

His father's calm face gave no hint of the long talks with his wife as David lay asleep after his hours of hauling. "Sometimes good men make bad mistakes," he said. "It takes character, David, not to become bitter when you are falsely accused."

David mopped at his damp forehead. "But suppose I never do find out who robbed those traps? Whoever did it has stopped, for the time being, anyway. There just isn't any way to prove it, now, Dad."

Mr. Blake polished his glasses. "I thought that might happen."

"The men think I'm the thief. They're probably saying I stopped because of their warning." Despair shook the boy's voice.

"Fortunately," said his father clearly, "you haven't time for self-pity. Just keep on doing the best you can, and things will straighten out in time, son."

Time, thought David listlessly. Time could mean years and years. The sea, it was true, was as filled with wonder and beauty as it ever had been. But somehow the challenge had gone from it. Whether he did well or poorly seemed to matter less with each passing day.

His thoughts were interrupted when Sally, doing the dishes with her mother, called him to the telephone.

"Hurry up!" she cried. "It's Poke, and he sounds sort of queer."

It was Poke's voice all right, unnaturally tense, and so hurried that David strained to hear. "I'm down at the yacht club waiting on tables," said Poke. "Can you hear me?"

"Sure," said David.

"Get on your bike and come down here fast."

"Tonight? Now?" David broke in, surprised.

112

"Tonight. Now. Roddie just made a big scene over
dessert. It began when someone asked him about his
lobster business. Roddie said he had been top man for
weeks and had made a pot of money."

"Top man!" said David in bewilderment. With only
eight or ten traps? He listened and his heart began to
pound.

"Then Mr. McNeill made a remark about how the
successful people stay on top once they get there. He
asked Roddie what had happened lately, since he was
bringing in only enough lobsters for a couple of tea
sandwiches. He meant it as a joke, I think, but Roddie
was hot and he said too much. He said that his father
knew nothing when it came to lobstering. Roddie

113

claimed he could be top man again any time he liked. Mr. McNeill turned as purple as a grape and told him to prove it if he wanted to keep his fancy boat."

David whistled.

"Then Roddie shouted, 'I'll prove it, right now! I'll be back before the dance is over, and I'll have a couple of dozen!' And he slammed out of here and headed for the float." Poke paused for breath. "Listen!"

David could hear the mingled sounds of voices and laughter, then the faint beat of a motor.

"Poke," he cried, "Roddie can't count on getting a couple of dozen from his own traps, or even half that many!"

"Exactly what I thought," said Poke. "But nobody here knows that. If you're waiting at the yacht club for him when he comes in, perhaps you can start a few people thinking . . . ."

Swiftly David made up his mind. "Meet me at the town landing, Poke. Not the yacht club. The town landing!" he repeated clearly before he broke the connection.

Then he turned to Sally. "Tell Dad I'm off for town. And tell him," he called back over his shoulder, "I think we've got us a lobster thief!"

Cutting through the kitchen, David lost no time in getting his bicycle out of the barn. Then, head low and heart racing, he headed for town. It was not until he rattled across the wooden bridge over Goose Creek that he was aware of something behind him.

He threw a quick glance over his shoulder. There was Sally, pigtails flying, pedaling for all she was worth.

114

Chapter

8

THE BIG BLOW

TIME was running out. There was no time to stop, no time to argue the matter. Without a word, the two sped on and the hot evening air winged against their faces. Low in the south the heat lightning flared, and now and then thunder rumbled long in the distance.

One by one they passed the familiar landmarks — the salt marsh, the spruce woods, the dim fields alight with fireflies. Breathing hard, they pushed their bicycles up the hill past Lookout Rock. With the wind whistling in their hair they coasted down Harbor Road, then through Main Street and onto the dock.

Poke was waiting at the town landing.

"Roddie just went around Grindstone Point," he reported. "And so far, he's been hauling only his own traps."

Sally was still breathless from her ride to town. But she was beginning to understand and her eyes were wide with wonder. "What are we going to do?" she panted.

"We're going to catch a fox," Poke told her gravely. "But Fishermen's Dock is the last place Roddie will land with a load of illegal lobsters. Why didn't you two come over to the yacht club?"

"Because I'm going out," said David, already untying the *Lobster Boy's* bow line. "This is what we've been waiting for, Poke. And with or without the warden, I'm going to catch Roddie in the act of hauling someone's traps."

"Without another witness," Poke said slowly, "it will be your word against Roddie's."

David looked up at his friend. "Will you come, Poke?"

Without answering, Poke moved toward the dory. Then he faltered and stopped. His face was pale in the dusk, his dark eyes tortured.

"I can't," he whispered.

Only Sally standing beside him heard, and pity for him tightened in her throat. At the same time she had no intention of being left behind.

"David Blake," she said clearly. "I've pedaled all the way to town and I'm as hot as a baked potato, and I'm coming out with you myself."

"Then get in and push her off." Anger with Poke, and something more than anger, made David's voice short. He had already uncovered the motor, had swiftly checked it. Now, his lips locked tightly together, David took up the oars without another glance at his friend.

From the bow Sally looked back at the lanky figure standing on the float. Poke stood shamed and hurt, as if someone had struck him hard.

It was Poke who told us about Roddie tonight, she thought miserably, and we didn't even say thank you. But now it was too late. They were already too far from the dock.

Sally moved her legs over the thwart and faced the long cove. Somewhere out there was Roddie. She leaned forward as if to move the dory faster by her eagerness. "Can't we use the outboard yet?" she asked.

"We don't want him to hear us," said David in a low voice. "The motor's ready if we need it."

Sally nodded, and excitement mounted inside her.

"If Roddie robs any traps," David continued, "he'll probably haul those near the ledges where it's darkest. So keep your eyes and ears open and don't talk, especially when he cuts back his motor to haul."

David pulled steadily at the oars. Past the silent shapes of lobster boats they moved, under the taut anchor lines of the schooners. And always they kept well within the shadows. As if to aid them, the clouds had overspread the sky and blotted out the early stars.

They passed the yacht club, gay with music, dancing with lights. When they rounded Grindstone Point the lights disappeared behind them and the music faded, lost in the growing rumble of thunder.

Here by the ledges the buoys bobbed more plentifully. They glanced at them, wondering if Roddie had hauled them moments before.

And then they heard the slow beat of an idling motor.

"He's out beyond Blake's, I think," David said softly. He leaned forward on the oars to listen, to wait.

They were just off Tub Island. Sally caught the

glint of water from behind the solid cove which people called The Bite. A trick of the failing daylight, she thought. With the storm moving up, it would very soon be dark. If only, before it got any darker, they might witness Roddie hauling someone's traps. Then they could call in the warden and clear David of the charge against him. Then, at last, they would be free to search Tub Island for the treasure, just as they had planned to do that last happy morning in the fog.

The breathing of the sea was more restless now. A nervous little wind ruffled the bay. The first raindrops began to fall, cooling their hot faces and dampening their hair. David pulled the oilskins from underneath the seat and they shrugged into them.

"Life jacket, too, Sally," he said.

She caught the hated garment and tied it on. Then, facing the bay, she started. "There he is!"

Beyond the shelter of Blake's Island the *Pirate* was nosing into view, pitching in the rougher water. And Roddie McNeill, bared to the waist, was hauling in a trap.

"That's Willie Greenlaw's," David whispered. Silently, they watched as Roddie, working fast, emptied the trap and tossed it unbaited back into the water. Then came the powerful throb of his motor as the *Pirate* swung toward them.

Sally cried, "David, he'll see us!"

But Roddie merely completed his turn and headed toward the traps set near The Graves.

"Hurry up and follow him." Sally stirred restlessly on the seat.

But David shook his head. "The dory wouldn't like it out there now." The rising wind threatened to blow off David's sou'wester. Impatiently, he cast it underneath the seat and took up the oars again. "We've seen what we came to see. We'd better get back." Glancing once more toward the *Pirate*, he suddenly narrowed his eyes against the rain.

"The fool! He isn't stopping at The Graves, Sally. He's making for Perce's string out off Little Fox."

"Well, what do we care?" Sally snapped. She was beginning to feel wet and very uncomfortable.

"The tide is coming in and there's an offshore wind," David told her bluntly. "Outside the tide rip that means trouble."

He was already rowing back. "He'll probably be all right, but I'm going to keep an eye on him. I'm putting you off at Blake's, Sally."

The girl was silent with horror. Alone on the island? And in a thunderstorm at night?

"You'll be all right. Just go up the path the way we did before. The door's unlocked and the candle is on the sink. You can even light a fire and get dried out."

Bleakly, Sally watched the island cove draw near. David was counting on her, she thought. If Roddie needed help, then her extra weight in the dory would be a danger. Her chin went up and she managed a shaky grin.

"Good girl." David guided the dory into the cove and held it steady as Sally leaped out. He waited for a moment to watch her struggle up the wet path in the dusk. With a wave, she disappeared into the spruces.

Then David headed the dory seaward. He kept just inside the tide rip, where merging currents formed a long and evil ribbon of froth. Often before, fascinated, he had watched the little whirlpools, spinning and funneling downward from the surface. Now he feared their trickery.

Here, protected by the island, the dory rose and fell in comparative calm. But beyond the tide rip lay the bay, its seas running high before the storm wind. Here he would stay, David decided. He had no wish to do battle in the dory with his enemy, the wind.

The *Pirate* had beat her way to the traps set in the lee of Little Fox Island. As Roddie cut back the motor she was pitching steeply. Yet even now it seemed that he would complete his work with nothing worse than a drenching from the rain.

But then David strained forward. Roddie was having trouble with the trap. Holding the line in both hands, he was seeking a firm stance for hauling. Then on a steep wave the *Pirate* reared to one side. For a moment the boy struggled for balance and then went over, arms flung wide, into the sea.

In one motion David drew in the oars and sprang to the outboard.

Let her start right up, he prayed. He pulled the cord once, twice. *Let her start!* The motor caught, and David held to the stick as the *Lobster Boy* entered the tide rip.

Snarling jaws seemed to tear at her, turning her first one way, then another. But slowly the dory struggled ahead, into the steep seas beyond.

In a flash of lightning David caught a swift vision of Roddie in the water beside the *Pirate*. With both hands he had gripped the gunwale of the tossing boat and was clinging onto it desperately.

"Hang on," David called, and his words fell like whispers into the shouting wind.

He had opened the motor wide and the dory surged ahead. Up each black hill of water she throbbed. Then, lifted forward on a following sea, she plunged down, down, her motor gasping. On through the rough water of the bay she labored. As the distance between them narrowed, the lightning flared again. David saw by the sharpened set of Roddie's face that the boy could not hold out much longer.

He nosed dangerously close to the *Pirate* and swung as much of his weight to starboard as he dared. Then, leaning forward, he thrust a wet hand toward Roddie.

The boy grasped and missed, lost his hold on the gunwale and went down. Then, kicking hysterically, he rose again to the surface. In another moment, David knew, the two boats would close together. He watched the approaching wave mount to its peak, fall, swing the dory alongside the *Pirate*. Swiftly, he hooked a leg under the seat, and leaning over, seized Roddie by the shoulder.

The boy struck out blindly, seeking a hold on David, on the dory, on anything solid in this cold nightmare of rushing water.

"Help me!" David cried between clenched teeth.

With a final, heartbreaking effort he half hauled, half lifted Roddie into the dory where the boy sprawled, spent and gasping, across the seat.

Then the sea, like a mighty arm, thrust against them and over them. It spun the dory half about and carried her swiftly on past the larger boat. The two boats had not come together. They still had a chance.

"Get down," panted David.

Weakly, Roddie dragged his legs off the thwart. Then he lay back, sobbing, on the bottom of the boat.

The little dory was bucking like a whipped colt, and David gave her his whole attention. Opening the throttle, he made a careful arc around the *Pirate*. Behind them the new boat tossed helplessly, riding the waves and the wind straight to her doom on the ledges of Little Fox Island.

Roddie raised his head. "The boat . . . ." he gasped.

"Can't help it," David shouted.

Then he ignored Roddie and turned his face toward Blake's Island and safety.

Although the rain beat through their thin clothes more heavily than ever, the squall wind had weakened. Wearily, David held the dory on her homeward course, back through the boiling tide rip to the calmer water of the cove.

Roddie, his eyes tightly closed, held fast to the slats on the dory's bottom. It was only when David cut off the motor that he opened his eyes again. Then, slowly, he struggled up out of the dory to help David beach the *Lobster Boy* in the driving rain and the darkness.

David waited through a roll of thunder that seemed

to tear from the very heart of the island. Then he demanded, "Why did you go outside on a night like this?"

"That's my business," said Roddie bitterly. "What are we doing here? Why don't we go back to town?"

"And that's my business," David snapped. Then with a kindness which he could not have explained, he added, "My sister's waiting for me in the old house." He paused. "You coming?"

"No, thanks."

"You'll get soaked."

"That's my worry, isn't it?" Roddie was shivering uncontrollably. He lacked a shirt, and his pants clung wetly to his long legs. Yet David knew that he meant to remain here alone on the beach. Much in the same way David had remained alone with his own shame these past few weeks.

David took off his oilskin coat and threw it to Roddie. "Here. I can't be any wetter. This will keep the wind off."

Roddie caught it and tossed it scornfully into the dory.

David shrugged as he fought down his fury. Then he started up the path to the house.

Not so very long before, Sally, too, had come this way, reluctant, her head lowered against the storm. Just short of the house she paused. There it stood, rain-streaked and solitary, staring seaward like an old man with empty eyes.

"I won't go in there all alone," she decided. "I'll stand under something till David comes back."

On a gust of wind she heard the beat of his motor,

indistinct and uncertain. Ashamed, Sally thought of the real danger which her brother was at this moment facing for Roddie McNeill. David had said to wait for him in the homestead, so there she would wait.

She reached the house, and with some relief pushed open the door. As before the old kitchen was dark. It smelled musty and long closed. She left the door wide open and the rain blew in and pelted upon the floor.

"Now," she told herself very firmly, "all I have to do is find the candle." She made out the dim outline of the wooden sink. David had said the candle was here somewhere. Cautiously, Sally reached out an exploring hand and came into contact with a spiderweb. Swiftly recoiling, her hand hit the old candle bottle and sent it crashing into the sink.

Panic swept over her like a chill wind. Light! She must have some light! Sally was tense, her breathing harsh, when her hands found the match dish. In a moment her little candle flame was dancing in the draft. She hastened to close the door.

Then she threw off the bulky life jacket and sat on the nail keg where she had sat so many days before. Now, as then, the rain beat hard against the shutters. Just as before, the thunder crashed and crashed again and fled echoing down the cove. Then, however, it had been daytime, and David had been with her. But now the night was falling fast and Sally was alone before a cold hearth. She found herself holding her breath, eyeing the shadows in the still rooms beyond.

Then she leaped angrily to her feet. "You're a big

girl now, Sally Blake," she told herself. She started to lay a fire from the materials which David kept on hand in the wood box. "Think of something else. Think of David."

In the act of crumpling the paper, she paused to listen for the sound of his motor. She heard the restless wind driving the rain against the house; a chattering of thunder; and, borne on a gust, the faint tolling of the bell buoy out in the channel. But there was no sound of a motor. Crouched and tense, Sally pictured the old dory swamping in the bay and David struggling alone in the black water with nobody to help him. She caught her breath audibly. She must not think of David.

Think of the Blake treasure, then. Mechanically, Sally arranged the driftwood tepee-fashion, as her brother did. Somewhere on Tub Island was the treasure. That much they had decided that terrible day when the men had accused David of hauling their traps.

She remembered her walk home, despairing, from the dock, and her resolve to explore Tub Island all by herself if need be. But there had been no way. As she had feared, David had had no time, no heart, for the hunt.

But now there was a way — she was on Blake's Island at last. It was not yet high tide — the sand bar to Tub Island would be, for a little while, free. Only now, of course, she had to wait for David. Besides, it was raining very hard. It was not the time to explore.

Sally rose from her knees and brushed off her dungarees. Strange, she thought. The Bite, as they had rowed past it at dusk, had seemed to wink and twinkle with water, almost as though the tide were wearing away a little cave inside the ledge. It would take a long, long time, thought Sally, reaching for the matches, for the sea to wear away all that granite.

A quick little chill chased up her spine and she stiffened, forgetting the matches. Her mind did a dizzy somersault. What if there should be a tunnel there behind The Bite? Poke had told them something once about the tide making tunnels in the softer rock. Suppose, then, that there was such a tunnel on Tub Island, a tunnel where a treasure might be taken and hidden, and no one the wiser.

Sally shivered with excitement and hugged her arms. "If only I had a flashlight," she told herself, "I could cross the bar before the tide comes in and just take one quick look. Then when David gets back I might have the whole mystery solved all by myself. That would more than make up for losing Jonathan's old chart." Hopefully, she looked around the empty room, but there was only her little candle beside her on the hearth.

The buttery. There were lanterns stored in the buttery, she remembered. Snatching up the candle, Sally darted into the musty room. In triumph, she bore the largest of the lanterns into the kitchen and filled it from the can of kerosene left there by the lobstermen. She knew about oil lamps. Her mother kept them in the house in case the electricity went off during a thunderstorm. You turn up the wick, like this. Light it. Adjust it. There!

Sally snapped shut the door of the lantern and hurried out into the storm, leaving her life jacket behind her on the nail keg where, for a while, it continued to drip, forming a little puddle on the floor.

Down through the uncut island field went Sally, tall grass whipping about her legs and soaking her jeans. The field became an alder thicket, reaching with wet, laced fingers for her lantern. Then at last she was on the path that led through the spruces to the sand bar. Sally was grateful for the lightning now. It warned her of low-hanging branches that would wrench the lantern from her hand.

Ahead glistened the dark arm of the sand bar leading to Tub Island. Sally hurried across, holding the lantern high. Beneath her feet the narrow strip of sand was firm enough, but the dark water frothed and curled on either side.

"The tide is coming in," she warned herself. "But there's time to take a look at The Bite and get back again before the bar is underwater." She wished that she had thought to leave a note for David, but she hadn't had a pencil. Anyway, it was too late now to worry about it.

Sally was relieved to reach Tub Island. The Bite was not much farther from here. Outwardly, she was aware of the gravelly beach beneath her feet, of the storm and the sounds of the storm. Once she thought she heard the dim beat of an outboard motor nearby.

But more real and pressing than these things was her vision of a tunnel and, head down, she hurried on. She soon began to tire. It was not easy to climb over the slippery rocks and, at the same time, keep her lantern upright. Then she drew a sigh of relief. She had reached

The Bite, that boulder-cluttered nook of coast so familiar to everyone in Saturday Cove.

Tonight, however, there seemed to be more boulders than usual, and the ledge looked knife-sharp. Sally saw with triumph how now a narrow inlet flowed on behind the tumbled rocks. Half afraid, but too curious to turn back, she followed the shoreline into an opening between the ledges.

Then she stood and stared and stared. Here was a tunnel, just as she had thought. Here was a tunnel that must lead into the heart of Tub Island!

Chapter

9

TO CATCH A FOX

A FEW cautious steps, and Sally walked in a different world. In this place the wind did not exist. The voices of the storm and sea grew distant and were still. Overhead, ledge rock and tree roots formed a dark, fantastic roof, and at her feet the somber tide wound peacefully along. Beyond the light of the lantern the granite walls, the tide, were lost in blackness. The very air was hushed, as if time had just begun.

She was inside the island. Surely she had found the hiding-place of the Blake treasure!

Filled with wonder, Sally moved on, her lantern suddenly vital in this deep and nightbound cavern. At one point the tide thinned to a licking tongue and ended. Now, she could walk directly in the bed of the ancient creek. Eagerly, she studied the solid walls, the watermarks, the floor worn smooth by ancient tides. Surely this stone passage deep inside Tub Island was the best hiding-place in Saturday Cove. Perhaps, if the water was high enough, Jonathan had rowed his skiff up to this very spot.

131

After a while Sally sat down, placing her lantern carefully beside her. The boys would be proud of her. Why, she might even discover the treasure, just as she had found this tunnel, all by herself. Only where, in this passage of stone, could Jonathan have dug a hole and hidden anything?

The toe of her sneaker felt suddenly cold. Curiously, she glanced down to see the tide rubbing at her feet like a silent cat. With horror, she snatched up the lantern and sprang back. The water was rising. Already, it had covered an ancient mark which she had thought was the high water line.

She must get out of here! Downstream, the tide stretched wet and black toward the distant opening. She must reach the outside before it filled the entrance or she would be trapped in this place without a boat, without even a life jacket.

Sally ran unsteadily toward the opening. But the broad bank had narrowed. The swelling tide was already cutting her off. With a little cry, she swung around. Deep within the tunnel, perhaps, she could escape the oncoming tide. But would there be air at that inner end? It seemed that the heavy roof pressed down and down upon her, even as the tide reached hungrily upward.

Panic rose in her throat and she turned back toward the black mouth of the inlet. Better to return to the air, even if she must wade shoulder-deep to get out. Once Sally slipped and fell to her knees at the edge of the cold water. The lantern! She must keep it dry. Her arm ached and sobs caught at her throat. The

bank had narrowed to a ledge that disappeared just ahead beneath the water. In another moment she must enter the stream and start wading toward the opening.

Then she saw something strange and unreal. There seemed to be two eyes of fire that moved slowly toward her out of the mouth of the channel. She froze in a crouching position. Nightmare visions of a sea monster sprang into her mind. Now, she heard the stealthy sounds of its movement through the water.

With a chill of fear she realized that her lantern gave away her position, and she hurled it from her. It fell with a hissing splash into the tide. Then she whipped about and was running, running. Losing her footing on the slippery bank, she clutched once at the darkness. Then she fell full-length into the black water. Coldly, it flashed over her head. Sally fought to the surface and screamed. Under again. Up again, choking for air. *Flatten out*, David had said. *Move your arms, kick your legs! Flatten out!* Desperately, Sally flattened her body, thrashed her arms and legs — and stayed afloat. She did not again go under. She stayed afloat!

But she seemed to keep on bumping against something. Panicking, she thought again of sea monsters. Which way was the bank?

She heard a voice calling again and again, "Sally! Sally! Over here!" With a sob of relief, Sally caught at something, an extended oar. She pulled herself up to the side of a boat. How odd that Poke should be here! And what was Poke laughing about at such a time?

"Sally!" Poke gasped. "Stand up! You're only in

about three feet of water. You're bumping on the bottom!"

Gingerly, Sally reached her feet down. Then she was standing by the dory, a miserable figure dripping fire in the darkness. "What makes me so shiny?" she said foolishly.

Poke smiled. "Phosphorescence. Tiny marine life that glows in the dark," he explained. "The water is full of it tonight." He reached out with both hands to help her into the dory.

Of course, thought Sally. What she had seen were the strokes of Poke's oars as he rowed toward her into the tunnel. "I thought you were a sea serpent," she cried, shivering.

Poke helped her into his jacket. "And I thought you were the ghost of Jonathan Blake, or I would have called out sooner."

He shone his flashlight over the walls that closed above them. Then he nodded. "Jonathan's hiding place, of course. We'll explore it tomorrow, you and David and I. How did you ever find it, Sally?"

Sally tossed her wet pigtails and sent a flaming shower over them both. "By detective reasoning," she told him.

"Deductive," Poke corrected. "Now, what happened?"

It was fun telling Poke about her trip across the sand bar in the storm and her discovery of Jonathan's tunnel. The approval in Poke's face made her feel very brave and very important. But in spite of being wrapped in Poke's warm jacket, Sally shivered as she described her flight from the rising tide.

Poke nodded thoughtfully. "I'm glad I frightened you back upstream, because the entrance is pretty deep. From the angle of this creek, though, I'd guess you would have been safe and dry a little farther up. Anyway," he finished, "you learned how to swim."

Sally gazed at him in amazement. "Swim! Was I swimming, Poke? In three feet of water?"

"It was not very graceful swimming. But you were keeping yourself up just as well as if you had had ten feet of water under you."

"Swimming!" Sally shook her head with delight. "I was swimming! But if you hadn't come along in a boat . . . ." She broke off and stared at Poke as if he were a vision. "You, Poke. *You came in a boat!*"

Poke stirred uneasily. "You're shivering. Let's get you home." He handed her the flashlight and took up the oars.

Sally shone the light down the eerie passage ahead, and they began the dark journey back through the heart of the island.

Then Sally's eyes narrowed as she studied the boy. "You handle a dory awfully well for someone who never goes near the water. I want to know about it," she told him bluntly.

"I thought you might," Poke said dryly. But the minutes went by as Poke seemed to consider how to begin. Strange shadows moved along the rock walls beyond the flashlight's beam. The water flowed past them as black as ink.

When he spoke again, Poke's voice echoed hollowly around them. "I used to live on the Cape," he began,

136

"before I came to Saturday Cove. I spent all the time I could around boats. We all loved the water, just as David does — Mom, and Dad, and my sister."

His sister! Poke had never spoken of a sister before. Sally nodded, without understanding.

"We had always owned a sailboat," Poke continued, "and that year we'd bought a new sloop, a forty-five footer." Again the look of tragedy touched the boy's face. Sally waited, saying nothing.

"She was a beautiful sailor, that boat. It wasn't her fault. We were caught in a squall that day around sunset. A sail got fouled up and Dad gave me the wheel and went to fix it. He gave *me* the wheel . . . ."

Poke had stopped rowing and the dory floated soundlessly on the flood tide. His voice had fallen so low that Sally scarcely breathed lest she miss his words.

"We were a long way offshore when she went over. So we stayed with the boat. We were out there all night. They found us the next day, Sally. I was the only one left."

Sally felt the tears sting into her eyes. She badly wanted to say something, but no words came. So this was the reason for Poke's hatred and fear of the water.

When Poke took up the oars again, his voice was more normal. "I should have told you and Dave before. But I had asked Uncle Fred not to talk about it around here. I wanted to forget about it."

Sally's eyes darkened with the thought of what this boy had gone through. Poor Poke, she thought. But she did not say it. It would be awful to be pitied all the time.

137

"I had to be near the water," Poke went on, "so Uncle Fred let me work around the Supply. And I wanted to get into a boat again. But somehow I never could, not even when David asked me to be his partner."

"What about tonight?" urged Sally.

"Tonight, when you two followed Roddie without me, I knew what David was thinking. He was thinking I was a coward."

"Oh, no, Poke! He wasn't!" But Poke ignored her.

"At first I didn't do anything. I just hung around, thinking about it. It was still light enough to see out on the water, so I went up to the Supply for the field glasses. I know where Willis Greenlaw has his string, and I saw Roddie hauling it."

"We saw him, too."

"I have an idea that Roddie had quite an audience," Poke added. "I thought that Uncle Charlie ought to know, so I telephoned the Lobster Pot."

Sally agreed eagerly. "Then, what?"

"Just before the squall hit, I saw Roddie going outside the tide rip toward Little Fox, and David head out after him. So then, of course," said Poke, "I called the Coast Guard."

"You what?" Sally cried in thrilled disbelief.

"I called the Coast Guard and they agreed to proceed with haste to Little Fox. After that all I could do was wait. It was dark by then and the storm closed in. I couldn't see what was happening. I could only think." The old despair touched the boy's face and Sally looked away.

"I kept thinking that I was nearer to David than the Coast Guard was. So," said Poke simply, "I came."

"How did you dare to do it, Poke?" she asked him timidly.

Poke looked at her. "The same way you learned to swim. You thought you had to."

Sally nodded, understanding at last. To follow Roddie, to clear David's name, had not been enough. Only fear for his friend's life was bigger than Poke's fear of the sea.

"By the time I reached Grindstone Point," Poke was saying, "the Coast Guard cutter was already out by Little Fox. I could see her searchlight through the rain. So I decided to go in at Blake's or Tub and wait out the storm. That was when I saw the light on the shore."

"My light!" Sally exclaimed. "Oh, Poke, I wish I had known you were there. It was scary coming in here all alone."

"It was scary for me, too. You looked like a ghost. First you were there, then you weren't. I had to find out, so I nosed in here after you."

"If you hadn't, I might have been drowned," Sally told him in a wondering voice. Then she had a thought. "Will it last, Poke? I mean, now that you're not . . . afraid any more, will you stay that way?"

Poke said slowly, "I'll stay that way, Sally."

Sally sighed, filled with content. Poke would be all right from now on. And she, at last, had learned to swim. Never again would she be treated like a baby in a boat. Dreamily, she gazed toward the entrance ahead, and her eyes widened. No longer was it the dim circle of light that it had been — it was now a pale arc. "Can we get out?" she asked uneasily.

Poke threw her an amused glance. "The tide is turning, Sally. It won't come any higher. We'll have to duck down, but we'll make it."

Poke shipped the oars and they got down carefully into the bottom. Then, with inches to spare, they moved outward on the current.

The squall had passed over. The night air was sweet and warm, and a full moon was rising out of the sea beyond Blueberry Island. Poke rowed past the boulders and well beyond The Bite before he shifted to the stern to start up the outboard.

"Listen," said Sally. "I heard someone call."

Across the water came a long "HALLOOOO."

"Blink the flashlight toward them," Poke ordered.

Sally did so, and almost immediately they were in the full glare of a searchlight.

Poke pulled the motor back up onto the stern board. "We're about to be rescued by the United States Coast Guard," he chuckled.

Out of the night came the pale, trim shape of the cutter with the little *Lobster Boy* in tow. Anxious faces peered down at them.

"That you, Sally?" It was David's voice, heavy with worry.

"It's both of us," said Poke.

"*Poke!*"

They heard David's exclamation of surprise, and a quick question that was lost as one of the seamen tossed

140

them a rope. "Tie up the dory," they were told. "Then pull her up alongside, and we'll get you aboard."

Soon Sally and Poke crowded into the little cabin, and the cutter got underway for Saturday Cove. But they could not talk freely to David yet. For Roddie sat apart in one corner, sullen-faced and silent, a blanket wrapped tightly about his shoulders in spite of the warm night. And a young seaman looking not much older than Poke, himself, stood grinning at them from the hatchway.

"Sally, what did you want to leave for?" David demanded. "I told you to wait for me in the house, and all I found when I got back was your life jacket messing up the floor. Not a trace of you anywhere," her brother went on angrily, "till the Coast Guard spotted that dory."

Sally glanced at Roddie. Much as she was longing to tell David of her discovery of the tunnel, she must not speak of it in front of Roddie. She yearned to tell him Poke's story, too. But not here. Not now.

"I just thought I'd take a little walk across the bar," she told him lamely.

The seaman threw back his head and laughed. "Man! How's that going to look in the report? 'Received call to rescue a couple of boys off Little Fox Island. Located them safe and sound on Blake's. Received information girl is missing off Blake's. Located girl and boy off Tub. Girl had gone for a little walk across the bar.'" The young man wagged his head.

But a little teasing could not bother Sally now, and she smiled back. She was too pleased to be near David again, to find him safe. "What happened after you went outside?" she asked her brother.

But David glanced at the seaman, then at Roddie, and slightly shook his head. His look said, Careful. Let's not tell the Coast Guard about Roddie's taking lobsters. He's in trouble enough as it is. Aloud he said, "Roddie and I made a mistake. We were out too far when the squall hit."

"Next time," the seaman said, "you boys better mind your storm warnings. If you're old enough to go ramming around in a boat, you're old enough to go by the rules."

142

"I guess that's right," said David agreeably.

Then, as if he had just noticed him, David looked directly at his best friend. "Hello, Poke."

Gravely, the two boys regarded each other. Something unpleasant clouded the air between them.

"This is the worst squall I've ever been out in," David said bluntly. "Yet here you are in the thick of it, in a dory smaller than mine. How come?"

Poke hesitated a little too long.

"I guess I wasn't supposed to believe all that business about you and the water, was I?" David said bitterly. "I guess that was all just kidding."

Silently Sally cried out, *Oh, David, no! Don't talk so! Poke lost his whole family in a storm like this!*

After a moment Poke shrugged and looked away. "I thought you might need me."

He missed the look that David sent him. It was an intent look of dawning respect, of growing gladness. Then David, ashamed of his outburst, wishing he could take back his words, studied the floor of the cabin.

Troubled, Sally looked from one to the other. After all that had happened, things ought to be turning out all right. But they weren't right at all.

The heavy silence was broken by a shout from one on the men on deck. "Make ready to bring her in!"

The cutter's engines slowed, went into reverse. The first to reach the deck, David stared landward in amazement. There, it seemed, was a large part of the town of Saturday Cove gathered at the dock.

In the moonlight their faces looked strained and worried. But when the children appeared at the deck rail a glad cry of welcome rose from them like a single voice. Some, David saw, were people from the yacht club in evening clothes. Others were townspeople attracted by the activity at the waterfront. All were equally wet and mussed.

There, too, stood Willis Greenlaw with the Dennetts and several other lobstermen.

Then he saw his parents. They were waiting anxiously at the ramp, side by side. Near them stood Poke's Uncle Fred and, yes, Mira Piper, hastily wiping her eyes.

Mr. and Mrs. Blake were the first to reach them, with a welcome so fervent that David said, embarrassed, "We're all right, Mom and Dad. We're okay. Just a little wet." Sally, calm though she had been aboard the cutter, unaccountably burst into tears. And off at one side, much to Poke's discomfort, Mira Piper was embracing him with all the affection of her motherly heart while Poke's Uncle Fred looked proudly on.

It was a moving scene in the moonlight. But David had a strange feeling that the people on the dock were waiting for something else. Something was unfinished. Something seemed to hang heavily in the warm night air.

Then Uncle Charlie pressed volubly toward them. "Whole durn town's been worried fit to bust," he shouted in a bellow that reached easily to Main Street. Only it seemed to David that the hearty voice was shaking a little.

The old lobsterman turned to the people. "Folks," he bugled, "thanks to the Coast Guard, these young'uns seem to be alive and kicking. Roddie McNeill, too, there inside the cabin."

He glanced over at Poke. "It was young Elijah Stokes called out the Coast Guard. I did, too, but he beat me to it. Then durn if that boy didn't head out there himself in a dory to see if he could help. Now that takes courage for anybody, and Poke never did like the water." Here cheers and applause interrupted Uncle Charlie. Poke stared hard at his shoes, greatly wishing to be elsewhere.

"But I got something else to say, 'fore we all go home, and this is the time and place to say it." Uncle Charlie cleared his throat and thought for a moment.

David saw Mr. McNeill push his way to the edge of the dock beside the cutter and then hesitate, waiting for his son to leave the cabin.

Uncle Charlie continued. "They's been some funny business going on around Sat'd'y Cove this summer. Seems someone ain't too particular about whose traps he's been haulin'." He glanced toward the lobstermen. "Sometimes folks who ought to know better make pretty bad mistakes. We made one about David Blake, some of us."

Startled, David muttered, "Please, Uncle Charlie."

Without flicking an eyelash, Uncle Charlie went on. "We told Dave he better quit haulin', 'fore he lost his license. But he knew he was innocent, and tonight he and his kid sister went out and got their proof." The old man ran a nervous finger inside his collar. Then he kept doggedly on.

"Just before the squall hit, Poke called me up over

to the antique shop. He says, 'If you want to know who's hauling illegally, take a look at the cove through one of those antique spy glasses of yours.' "

Then Uncle Charlie looked at Mr. McNeill and for a moment seemed to talk directly to him. "Now, I ain't saying who 'twas. Mebbe I don't need to. He won't even lose his license because the warden didn't catch him. But whoever 'twas, *it wa'n't Dave Blake!*"

Mr. McNeill glared at Uncle Charlie for a moment. Then without a word he stepped over onto the deck of the cutter and disappeared into the cabin.

Uncle Charlie took a deep breath, wrung David's hand, and made his way slowly across the dock to where his old car was waiting. It was getting along toward his bedtime.

A sigh, a murmur of talk, swept over the crowd. They began to break up into small groups, to move homeward, or to stop for a moment and congratulate the children on their safe return. Finally, as David and Sally and Poke started toward the parking lot with their families, Willis Greenlaw and the Dennett brothers caught up with them.

It was not easy for these men to make apologies.

"Things looked to be against you, Dave," Willis said uncomfortably. "You wouldn't speak up, you know."

"We don't feel very proud of ourselves," Foggy added, "and we'd somehow like to make it up. Perce, for instance, aims to keep you in bait, Dave, free for nothin', rest of the season."

"Why, Perce, you don't have to do that," said David.

"I know I don't," said Perce. "But I aim to do it just the same. So don't go spoiling my fun."

"I tied up your dory for you, down to the float," Willis added practically.

"Why, thanks, Willis." David wondered how he could have forgotten the *Lobster Boy*.

"Only," asked Willis, "how come the cutter didn't tow in Roddie's boat along with your dory?"

David hesitated.

"She must of got stove up, we're thinking," said Willis, "out there in that squall."

"What did you do, Dave," said Foggy after a moment, "pull that smart alec of a Roddie McNeill out the bay?" He stared at the boy wonderingly.

David nodded, and caught from his parents such a look of pride and love that he felt the color burn into his face.

Poke's dark eyes glowed with regard. He looked as if he would like to buff David warmly on the shoulder. But still he said nothing. David thought he was a coward or a liar. There was nothing to say.

They had reached The Sandwich Shoppe. Bidding the group good night, Willis and the Dennetts turned in for a mug-up of hot coffee. "Good haulin', pal!" called Foggy, and the door slammed cheerfully behind them.

David glanced up at the sky. It was a wonderful night! He was one of them again! But the world would not be right side up until he had settled something with Poke.

Side by side, a little behind the others, the two boys

walked together down Main Street. The parking lot was just ahead. There were too many things to say, thought David, and no time to say them.

He glanced at Poke. In the bright moonlight the strain of the past few hours showed plainly on the other boy's face. Painfully, David thought of the way he had left Poke tonight before the squall, in anger and without understanding. In spite of that, Poke had come out into the storm with the idea of helping him. David's heart was filled with pride in his friend.

"Poke?" David said.

The tall boy said nothing, waiting.

"I need a full-time partner, Poke. How about it? Will you come hauling with me?"

Poke thought for a moment. Then he turned and looked gravely at his friend. "When do we start?"

David drew a deep breath. "Tomorrow, bright and early," he said.

"Not tomorrow." Poke shook his head. "Because tomorrow you and Sally and I are going to unearth the Blake treasure — if there is one. How about the day after tomorrow?"

"It's a deal!" cried David.

The two boys gripped hands there under the quiet elms on Main Street.

Chapter

10

TWO KINDS OF TREASURE

IT was a day fashioned for a king. A brilliant blue day, so pure of air that Tub Island, set like a green jewel in the sparkling cove, seemed a stone's throw away.

The morning sun had not yet burned the dew off the grass by the gear shed when David and Sally and Poke arrived at Fishermen's Dock. Now they had only to refuel the outboard and load the dory and then, at last, be on their way to Jonathan's hiding place.

In high good humor David was kneeling on the stern seat, pouring fuel into the motor.

"Are you two sure you didn't dream up all this about a tunnel?" he asked. "Because you didn't need to, you know. Having Poke go partners with me is a plenty good excuse for a picnic."

Poke held the dory steady against the float. "You will have to see for yourself," he said calmly.

David laughed. "You bet I will." But there was a note of excitement in his voice that acted like a match to Sally's smouldering impatience.

"Oh, please, hurry up! We want to explore that whole tunnel before the tide comes in." Sally was seated on the edge of the float, dangling her brown legs in the cold water of the harbor.

Her brother screwed the cap back onto the fuel can. "Tide's high around eleven. That gives us 'most three hours."

"We may not need three hours," said Poke hopefully.

A cheerful voice interrupted him, and down the ramp came Mira Piper in a swirl of bright skirts. She had a large bakery box tucked under one arm.

"Now, don't look worried, because I shan't hold you up one minute." When she laughed her eyes crinkled up and she suddenly looked quite pretty.

"You're not holding us up, Miss Piper," said Poke loyally.

"Not 'Miss Piper,' please, Poke. After all we have been through together — barrels of rose fertilizer, musty old records, lost buttons, rescues at sea — I think you three should just call me Aunt Mira."

Lost buttons! David had forgotten the old pewter button missing from the historical collection.

"I've brought something for your picnic," she went on. She gave Poke a special smile as she handed him the box. "A dozen chocolate cream puffs."

The children's response was wholeheartedly noisy, but it seemed to please her, for she looked at them with fondness. "Just one more thing. Don't be too disappointed if you shouldn't find any treasure. You already have one, you know." Her quick gesture indicated either the cove or the beautiful day ahead of them,

or perhaps both. Then she turned to leave just as Uncle
Charlie trotted down the ramp.

Behind him, somewhat timidly, came Mrs. McNeill,
then Roddie, his face a blank, and finally Mr. McNeill
who seemed, for him, a little subdued.

"Gorry-mighty, what a pretty day," bellowed Uncle
Charlie to anyone concerned.

Aunt Mira smiled and started to answer. Instead, she
remained silent, staring dumbly at an ornament which
Roddie's mother wore around her neck. David followed her gaze.

It was a button on a silver chain. A very old pewter button, once sewn to the homespun coat of a minute-man. It had been lovingly polished and Mrs. McNeill wore it with pride.

Noting Aunt Mira's interest, she said, "It's lovely, isn't it? My son found it for me." She smiled shyly around at the group. "It's quite rare, you know. A Revolutionary War button."

There was a moment of painful silence. Roddie had gone very pale underneath his tan.

Then Aunt Mira rose nobly to the occasion. "It's the most interesting button that I have ever seen," she said in her clear voice. "You must value it very highly, especially since your son gave it to you." Then with a cordial nod, she mounted the ramp and disappeared beyond the dock.

David released his breath. Thoughtfully, he stored the picnic hamper underneath the bow seat. Poke just as thoughtfully added the spade and crowbar to the gear at the bottom of the dory. Sally clambered aboard with a flash lantern of Mr. Blake's and the box of cream puffs.

Uncle Charlie shouted, "Where you young'uns off to now?"

"A picnic," said Sally with a quick glance at Roddie.

Uncle Charlie chuckled. "A spade-and-crowbar pic-nic, if you ask me. Favorite sport 'round Sat'd'y Cove since Jonah was knee-high to a flounder," he told the McNeills.

"Maybe it won't be much longer." David shot an affectionate smile at the old man.

"Mebbe not," roared Uncle Charlie. He untied his old punt which was moored alongside the *Lobster Boy*. Then, to David's surprise, he said, "Come on, Rod."

Mrs. McNeill said quietly to Uncle Charlie, "First, let me thank you for taking Roddie out hauling with you. He needs any information you can give him. He must pay for his new boat with what he makes lobstering."

"And if you know what's good for you, Roddie," his father said heavily, "you'll do it in record time."

Roddie remained silent, but Mrs. McNeill shook her head. "No, Thomas. Roddie is going to learn this business thoroughly, without short cuts. In fact, I am wondering if Mr. Blake will act as a paid tutor to Roddie in his spare time, and teach him the things he needs to know in order to be safe on the water."

"Agreed! It's a deal," bugled Uncle Charlie. " 'Course I might give him some pointers on a few things besides how to haul," he said, rubbing his chin. "Only I'll throw them in free." He turned to Roddie. "Into the punt with you, Rod, and mind you step into the middle of her. When we git back in from haulin', I'll show you what to do about torn potheads and broken laths. After last night we'll have a plenty of 'em."

As Roddie crossed the float he pulled something from his pocket and handed it to David. "I picked this up in the cove a while back. It was floating on a batch of rockweed," he said awkwardly.

It was Jonathan's chart, water-stained but in fair condition. Now that they had no need of it, it would make a fine souvenir for Sally.

Roddie gave David a long look and said, "Thanks. Thanks for everything."

Thank you for saving my life, said Roddie's look. And for not giving me away about the button.

David nodded and put the chart into his pocket.

Then, carefully, Roddie rowed the punt out into the harbor with Uncle Charlie seated on the stern seat, puffing away at his pipe.

As Mr. McNeill turned to leave he said to David, "Roddie's mother and I don't know how to thank you for what you did last night. But we'll find a way to do so, soon."

And Mrs. McNeill touched David's sleeve in a kind of apology. "Roddie did a terrible thing, and we can never really make it right to you. But he has learned his lesson." Then she smiled at David in spite of the quick tears in her eyes. "Someday, perhaps, you two can be friends."

Then the McNeills mounted the ramp and were gone.

"And that," said Poke softly, "is that."

David took his place at the outboard and Poke pushed the dory away from the float. The strip of water widened behind them and the sea gulls wheeled overhead, and Sally sang with great heart:

"Cape Cod cats they have no tails,
Heave away! Heave away — !
They lost them all in sou'east gales,
We are bound for Califor-ni-ay!"

David and Poke came in for the chorus. "Heave away, my bully, bully boys," they sang to the steady beat of the motor. "We're bound for Califor-ni-ay!"

Speedily, David hauled several of his traps set close to the ledges off Grindstone Point. Soon there were enough lobsters in the picnic kettle to satisfy the grandest appetites. Then he turned the bow of the *Lobster Boy* toward Tub Island.

"About that button business," Poke said suddenly. "I think Aunt Mira was great not to tell the McNeills that Roddie took the button. They have enough to live down, as it is."

"I think so, too," Sally nodded earnestly. "Even if Roddie does get away with it."

David was thoughtful. "I don't think Roddie wants to get away with it. There was a look on his face, back there. I bet he'll try to make it up to Miss — to Aunt Mira, somehow."

"Perhaps there is hope for Roddie, after all," mused Poke. "Uncle Charlie seems to think so."

David chuckled. "Uncle Charlie will teach Roddie McNeill a whole lot more than just hauling." Unconsciously he straightened his shoulders. He felt, all at once, rid of a burden that he had carried since first meeting Roddie here in the cove.

Straight ahead lay Tub Island, comfortable and familiar. But today it was also mysterious, a secret waiting to be shared.

At their approach the long-necked cormorants rose screaming from the ledges. Swiftly, the great birds circled in the sunlight and flapped away toward The Graves.

David nosed the dory at low throttle into The Bite. He threaded a course among the boulders that cluttered the little cove. Then, carefully and without speaking, they entered the tunnel.

As they moved inward on the dark water, David looked wonderingly at the knife-sharp ledge, at the newly-fallen boulders on either side of the opening. So this dim passage had always been here, and no one ever had known of it. No one except Jonathan and his father, long years ago before the tunnel was blocked.

His voice echoed when he spoke. "I think I see what happened. Some storm recently rolled aside the boulders that sealed off this tunnel. And it must have been another storm that caused a cave-in and sealed it up in the first place, so that no one ever knew it was here."

"The very storm," said Poke with certainty, "that struck the cove the night of the British raid."

Sally's voice was hushed. "So that's why Jonathan and his father couldn't get their treasure again. There was a cave-in that night . . . ."

They glanced behind them at the rocks that still partly blocked the entrance. Beyond, the water sparkled in the sun, but within the tunnel it was somber, forbidding.

David pulled the motor onto the stern board. For some distance they poled up the channel in silence.

Then Poke said, "They must have hoped that the tides and storms would open the tunnel again, sooner or later. Possibly, they even tried to pry their way in. They waited all their lives, in a way, for the storm that didn't come in time for them."

"And they kept their hiding place secret while they waited," David pointed out. "And then Jonathan died before he told anyone."

The dory grated suddenly on the bottom of the channel. First ashore, Poke tied a line to the boat and payed it out as they moved up the tunnel. Just beyond the tide mark, he knotted it to an oak root that thrust out of the earth.

"Just in case we find — something, and forget to move the boat," he said.

David smiled his approval. Poke was a true seaman.

The three walked on deep into the tunnel, David leading the way with the flash lantern. At first the creek bed was smooth and level, but soon it became rocky and more inclined. Now and then they ducked their heads to avoid a low-hanging rock section of roof.

Once, in the murky gloom, Sally felt again last night's quick panic. She glanced back at the dry channel, half expecting to see the tide slowly rising around her feet.

Up ahead, David lifted the lantern high into the air and peered around. "Where shall we start to dig?"

They considered the tunnel, its rocky floor and walls, the network of roots and stone that formed its roof.

Poke shook his head. "There's no place to dig here."

"It's farther up. I know it," Sally declared. "I feel it in my bones."

157

"That's reason enough," said Poke. "Lead on, Dave."

Sally followed the boys. Almost, it seemed to her that she could see a boy in homespun, poling his skiff on a long-forgotten tide deep into this hideaway. She could almost hear the phantom whisper of his oar in the water.

Young Jonathan, his tawny hair tied back in the fashion of the day, would look tired. He had rowed hard across the bar in a rising wind, and beyond the brave, pale circle of his lantern, other dangers waited.

Sally said dreamily, "He must have hurried. He must have been worrying something awful about his family."

"Who must?"

"Jonathan. With the British in his house he would have hurried back to Blake's just as soon as he could. He'd have watched the house, maybe from behind the barn, till the British left."

"He had another reason for hurrying, too," David reminded them. "There was a bad storm coming up. Maybe he didn't even stop to bury the things. Maybe he thought that this tunnel was enough of a hiding place."

Now it was Poke's turn to carry the lantern. He considered the tunnel thoughtfully. "I know what he would have done. He would have put the things up high where they would be safe from the water."

David's eyes, too, roamed the walls. "Maybe on a ledge or something. Then he would have hurried back home. And except for the cave-in, he could have gotten

the stuff again in the morning as easy as rolling off a greased log."

"That's it," said Poke softly. "Look for a ledge."

They followed the moving ray of the torch into the twisting passageway ahead.

"It's growing steeper," David whispered.

"What are we whispering for?" whispered Sally.

"Sh," said Poke. "Look here!"

Bent low, they followed him around a bend and came abruptly into a deep and well-like cave worn almost circular by some ancient whirlpool. They straightened their backs and looked around them in awe. The roof arched high above their heads, lost in darkness. The lantern threw towering shadows headlong across the smooth walls. It was like walking unexpectedly into a cathedral.

"You see?" Poke whispered, excited. "This is a big pothole. Some underground waterfall wore it away long before Jonathan's time, perhaps when Tub Island was still part of the mainland."

But the history of this strange place did not interest David now. He shook his head, bitterly disappointed. "This is the end of the tunnel. These walls are 'most as smooth as an aggie. There's no place here to hide anything."

"Yes, there is," Sally told him firmly. "Jonathan left it here, somewhere high up. I have a feeling . . . ."

They scanned the walls above their heads. Then David mounted a tiny ledge. "Hand me the lantern, Poke," he said tersely. He took the light and shone it into an ancient crevice.

After a long moment he turned and slid back down. An odd smile of triumph played about his face.

"It's there, all right," he told them unevenly. "Take a look."

Poke boosted Sally up. With eyes as round as saucers she gazed upon a huge iron kettle wedged into a fault in the solid rock. Its lid was rusted tight. But it rested as securely in its hiding place as when Jonathan had covered it and left it there close to two centuries before.

Then it was Poke's turn. He stared at the kettle, tried without success to move it, and finally slid down. "Jonathan could never have lifted it up here, filled. He must have emptied it, put the kettle up, then filled it again piece by piece."

In a frenzy of curiosity, David leaped onto the ledge and tugged. "It won't budge," he said, panting.

"I'll get the crowbar," Poke called, bearing away the light.

As they waited in the heavy darkness, David lighted matches from the supply in his pocket.

"Except for you, Sally," he told his sister generously, "we might have turned back before we reached this cave. Sometimes I think you have second sight."

Sally shivered with excitement. "Sometimes I think so, too." She glanced over her shoulder. But the brave boy, Jonathan, had disappeared into the long shadows behind them. Instead, in the welcome light of the lantern, Poke returned with the crowbar.

For a time the boys took turns prying. They worked until the perspiration ran down their faces and their muscles turned to water. At last, breathless and panting, they looked at each other.

"It won't budge."

"It's part of the rock. We'll never get it out."

In a taut voice Sally asked, "Can't you just pry off the lid?"

David leaped again onto the ledge with the crowbar. For a few tense moments he wrestled with the lid. The harsh grating of iron against iron filled the cavern.

Then came a wrenching sound and David cried, "I've got it!" He worked out the bits of broken lid and then paused, looking in upon the contents.

"What's in there, David?" Sally whispered.

David moved things around with a dull clatter. "Lots of things." He was surprised to find that his voice and hands were shaking, his legs felt boneless.

Poke laughed in triumph. "Hand it all down and let's get it out into the sun."

The three hurried to remove the contents of the kettle to the floor of the cave, and then down the tunnel to the water's edge, with hands filled and pockets bulging. Loading the valuables into the dory was an exciting task since they paused to glance, however briefly, at each long-concealed object.

There was a pitcher, dull with age, whose beauty of design was not entirely hidden. There was a broad silver bowl to match. There were pewter plates and porringers, and a pewter teapot with its wooden finial partly rotted away. There was a jewel case containing a few gold rings and earrings and a locket that delighted

162

Sally with its quaint design. There were several tiny painted miniatures of early Blakes in the dress of the eighteenth century. There was a round wooden box filled with buttons. And finally, in a rotted leather pouch, lay a small pile of coins.

The light of the flash lantern was growing dim when Poke pushed the loaded dory afloat. With their treasure safely stored on David's old sweater at the bottom of the boat, they made their way through the dark tunnel and out into the sunshine.

At first nobody spoke. There were too many wonderful things to think about. On the little beach beside The Bite they made the *Lobster Boy* fast. Then, unloading the picnic things, they all began to talk at once.

"The more I think about it, the more certain I am that's a Paul Revere pitcher," Poke declared. "It's exactly like one that I once saw in a museum."

"Could be. And I want to find out more about those old coins." David placed the box of cream puffs carefully on the sand beside the picnic hamper.

"Did you see that beautiful gold locket?" Sally asked. "Inside there's a picture of a little boy," she went on softly. "I think it's Jonathan Blake when he was little."

"There may be some pewter buttons in that wooden box," Poke continued. He handed out the picnic kettle filled with its restless catch of lobsters. "In those days," he told them in his lecture voice, "buttons were very rare. The colonists made some out of pewter and some out of bone. A very few people were lucky enough to own silver ones brought from England."

163

David teased, "All this must be from the B's in your encyclopedia."

"Right," Poke agreed. "And Aunt Mira and Uncle Charlie will turn themselves inside out if you have any pewter buttons. As for silver ones!" He whistled softly.

"Let's have a look!" David reached into the dory toward the little wooden box.

"Not until we start the lobsters." Sally was matter-of-fact. "I want to see that treasure just as much as you do. But I'm hungry enough to eat a bear."

Agreeably, the boys combed the shore for driftwood. Sally spread the old picnic cloth on the little sunny beach that flanked the rocky entrance to the tunnel. Soon the fire was crackling. The lobsters and the

new corn steamed in the kettle. Then they opened the button box and emptied its contents out upon the picnic cloth.

"Sally Blake's buttons," mused Sally as she helped spread them around. Then she straightened. "Pewter! Lots of them! Just like the one Roddie took for his mother. Oh, David, Poke, let's give one to Aunt Mira. And one to Uncle Charlie, too."

"How about one for Mrs. McNeill?" David teased.

"Oh, yes! That will make her happier."

David said nothing, but he glanced with pride at his young sister.

"Here are some oval buttons," Poke announced. "Uncle Charlie once told me they are as scarce as dinosaur eggs."

David was scratching with his knife at several of the larger buttons, dull and crusty with mold. "What do you know? These things are silver, with designs and initials on them."

Poke whistled. "Do you realize," he asked in his sober way, "that the Blake treasure might really be a treasure, after all?" He stretched his long limbs and rose to peer into the lobster kettle.

Sally trotted after him. "They're beginning to look nice and red. What do you think, Poke?"

But Poke's answer, whatever it might be, was lost to David. The sand was warm beneath his shirt. He lay on his stomach and looked across the water toward his beloved island. He was seeing a brave boy his own age, rowing hard in a night wind with a covered iron kettle in the bottom of his boat.

Then the friendly phantom vanished and the world flooded in upon him. The waves lapped against the beach. A gull called and called in the noon-bright sky. The shining sand at his feet gave way to the silver water of the cove, and on the shore at Blake's the beach grass shone golden in the sun.

Aunt Mira was right. Here was the real treasure — the islands, the sky, the sea reaching out to the blue edge of time.

David turned over and stretched on his back, the sun hot on his eyelids. It was a moment of fulfillment. The treasure was found, Saturday Cove's old secret was now known and understood. All the nightmare trouble with the lobstermen was over. Best of all, Poke, his fear of the sea mastered, was David's partner in the wonderful business of lobstering.

'My cup runneth over,' thought David. Life had nothing more to offer. . . .

"David, wake up." Poke nudged him gently.

David struggled up onto one elbow to see Poke and Sally laughing good-naturedly at him. The picnic cloth was laden and the air was rich with the fragrance of good food. There were scarlet, steaming lobsters and piles of golden corn streaming with butter. Paper plates crowded with fat tomatoes and crisp cucumbers fresh from the garden. A new loaf of Mrs. Blake's yeast bread. A fat jug of icy lemonade. And Aunt Mira's box of cream puffs.

David sat up and grinned. I was wrong, he thought. Life does have more to offer!

"This," he said to Poke and Sally as he reached for a lobster, "is only the beginning."

ABOUT THE AUTHOR

Barbee Oliver Carleton was born in Thomaston, Maine, "of a Ship's Log and a Latin Grammar," she writes, "the ancestral stock being sea captains, teachers, and island builders of ships."

At the age of ten she wrote a book of children's verse, which far from making her rich and famous merely cost her mother postage to and from publishers. At Wellesley College she majored in English, became a member of the newspaper staff, and contributed to college publications. She was a recipient of the Masefield Prize for Poetry.

After graduation she became a high-school English teacher in Caribou, Maine. For a time she held an editorial post with Houghton Mifflin Company, but this ended with her marriage to an aeronautical engineer from Maine.

Now she lives north of Boston with her husband and two children, and spends her summers in a Maine fishing village. She is the author of *The Wonderful Cat of Cobbie Bean, Benny and the Bear,* and over eighty stories which have appeared in *Highlights for Children, Child Life,* and *Jack and Jill.*